D0276504

A

D

THE FLAYED DOG

CHANADON PUBLICATIONS LTD
PO Box 37431, London N3 2XP
www.chanadon.co.uk

First English language edition
Published by Chanadon Publications Ltd 2004

ISBN   0-9541973-3-X

Copyright © Christo Saprjanov

The author asserts the moral right to be identified as the author of this
work in accordance with the Copyright, Design and Patents Act 1988

All rights reserved. No part of this book should be reproduced, stored in
or introduced into a retrieval system, or transmitted by any form or
means (either electronically or mechanically, photocopied, recorded or
otherwise) without the prior express written permission of the publisher.
This book should not be lent, resold, hired out or otherwise disposed of
in any form other than that in which it is published.

135798642

A catalogue record of this book is available from the British Library

Formatted by Brewin Books Ltd, Studley, Warks.
Printed and bound by Janet 45, Bulgaria

Jacket imagery provided by Sandro Hyams
Designed by Alistair Brewin

F122,021
€19

GALWAY COUNTY LIBRARIES

THE FLAYED DOG

By

Christo Saprjanov

Chanadon Publications Ltd
London

GALWAY COUNTY LIBRARIES

To Guillermo Mejia

'All the generations of mortal man add up to nothing!
Show me the man whose happiness was anything more
than illusion followed by disillusion.'

From *King Oedipus* by Sophocles

'This is how a fool can't help
But pass his life in good repute;
He never needs to ask himself
Whether he's human or a brute.'

From *Stranger* by Hristo Botev
Translated by Kevin Ireland

'The living close the eyes of the dead;
The dead open the eyes of the living.'

Christo Saprjanov

ACCREDITATIONS

The Flayed Dog by Christo Saprjanov
translated by Katerina Popova

Adapted by James Holleyhead

Introduction by Aidan Rankin

Jacket imaging by Sandro Hyams

Design by Alistair Brewin

Introduction
By Aidan Rankin

(An analysis of the political background to the novel)

This brilliant, tense and intricately crafted little squib of a novel comes at a timely moment for readers in Western Europe. At a time when the European Union is expanding, in places, to the Russian frontier, the whole concept of Europe as we have understood it in the West is being revised from its roots. Or, to use a fashionable word, Europe is becoming 'inclusive'. This means that the Western – and especially Western intellectual – vision of Europe, has to be balanced against a very different world view, based on very different experiences, that is prevalent in the East. **The Flayed Dog** epitomises the Eastern European world view, or rather that aspect of the Eastern European world view that is most challenging to the West. In this respect, it is a para-political novel. It is not about politics, as such, but political and cultural questions pervade it.

The Flayed Dog is the product of Bulgaria, which straddles the borders of Europe and Asia; it is not a European Union member yet, although it aspires to be. It is a country too little known to the literary circles of the West, although it has produced much, a land of mountains, beaches, Orthodox male choirs of unsurpassed beauty and purity. But it was until recently orthodox in a different sense, being the most conforming of the Communist autocracies, the most subservient to the Soviet overlord. The speeches of Comrade Todor Zhivkov, its then leader, eulogies to soulless collectivism, are valuable as a parody of Marxist dogma, and reveal to us the hole in the heart of the left. During the late 1960s, a friend of mine drove through Bulgaria at the time of the May Day celebrations, en route to Turkey and Iran. He still recalls the red flags and banners, in ironic contrast to the stubbornly empty streets. For the Bulgarian people had, through ancient wisdom in part but also bitter experience, seen through the false ideals of their rulers. With a perspicacity that is light-years ahead of most Western intellectuals, even (perhaps especially) today, they had rejected ideological abstraction, with its inimitable blend of absurdity and cruelty.

Christo Saprjanov's novel expresses calmly and records that absurdity and cruelty, the black farce of 'really existing socialism'. It takes us into a world of forced labour, population transfers, ethnic and cultural cleansing, silly slogans about 'equality' (now more prevalent on American university campuses than in Eastern European states), hunger, bitterness, resignation, and ultimately, the triumph of the human spirit. This comes about through the sheer survival of individuals in these harsh conditions, ideological and physical. Yet it emerges as well in the persistence, within individuals, of bravery, generosity and kindness, of reaching out to others and retaining a sense of something outside the self, beyond the purely material. **The Flayed Dog** is therefore about the survival of the spiritual dimension in a brutal and materialistic wasteland. It is also about the superiority of love and friendship between real human beings over the abstract love for humanity on which totalitarianism is founded.

George Orwell once wrote of totalitarianism, whether of Right or Left, as the jackboot stamping on the human face forever. Totalitarian movements are superficially diverse, but share the same contempt for the individual, whether that is expressed in defining whole sections of the population as subhuman (as with the Far Right) or reducing whole categories of human beings to nameless, faceless members of 'minority groups' (as with the politically correct Left). As well as arbitrarily classifying human beings, totalitarians pit group against group – class against class, race against race, sex against sex. They devise mythical constructions of power which they hold responsible for the iniquities of the world: 'Jewish money power' for the Nazis, 'bourgeois hegemony' for the Marxists, black immigration for white racists, white imperialism for the non-white racists, 'the patriarchy' for feminists. Totalitarian thought processes of this kind balance the belief in demonic powers with an intense will to power of their own and a belief in their own version of the perfect and the pure. These visions are larger than the individual and so the lives and the welfare of the individual human beings are secondary to the collectivist 'project'. Totalitarianism is a thoroughly modern phenomenon, rooted in urban mass societies equipped with technology, a strident secular tendency in which the soul is denied. But at the same time, totalitarianism expresses the most primitive and superstitious aspect of the human psyche, playing upon the most basic impulses of fear and domination, anger and greed, sentimentality and cruelty. This is the paradox of totalitarianism's appeal to intellectuals, which Orwell recognised and feared. In totalitarian movements, the extremes of rationalism and irrationalism intersect. Totalitarianism is the backdrop to **The Flayed Dog.** In this case, it is Stalinist totalitarianism, although, it could just as easily be National Socialist, or Trotskyist, or even 'Neoliberal' in character. The slogans are different, but the results are much the same.

The story of **The Flayed Dog,** and the story of Eastern Europe in the twentieth century, shows that totalitarianism might destroy millions, but it ultimately destroys itself. They show us that the best impulses in human beings can survive where the worst impulses in humanity prevail. In this sense, **The Flayed Dog** is at once a profoundly pessimistic novel and a story of great optimism, of light in the midst of darkness. More importantly for us as Western readers, it stresses the value of the human scale over the grandiose and the abstract. This reflects the experience of Eastern Europe, for nearly a century a social laboratory for abstract dogmas, fascist and Communist. There, distrust of the Big Idea is ingrained, through bitter experience and shattered illusions. In Eastern Europe, slogans of inevitable progress are viewed with suspicion, grand plans and 'projects' distrust or reviled.

It is in the West, by contrast, that many of the abstractions that point ultimately to totalitarianism still find favour. The pursuit of an elusive 'equality', in place of fairness and tolerance, and the classification of individuals by ethnic or cultural group are no longer the respective *preserves of Marxism and nationalism. Instead, they are both ingredients of a corrupt and mutant form of Western liberalism. This 'progressive' and collectivist mindset has risen to prominence both in Western Europe and in the United States, which although founded on the principles of individual freedom, is now increasingly the homeland of group rights. At the same time, some intellectuals who only a few years age clung tenaciously to Leftist dogma now espouse with equal fervour a form of free-market fundamentalism. This 'market forces' dogma has none of the intellectual rigour or complexity of Adam Smith. Instead, it is a mirror of the undergraduate Trotskyism of the 1960's, reducing the individual to a mere economic unit condemning us all to 'permanent revolution'.*

The Flayed Dog *shows us that the human being will always be more that an economic unit, that we are not plastic creatures that can be moulded by ideologies. It reminds us that there are ultimate truths that outlast propaganda and bad faith. As such, it is a novel whose time has come, for it contains within it a spiritual power the Europe needs.*

Economic Research Council
London
February 2004

Komi Autonomous Soviet Socialist Republic, a thousand kilometres north and east of Moscow. Taiga, swamps and night – white night. A train chugged by, snaking along its silver trail. It was an old train and knew the way well enough. The workers it carried were Bulgarians, and they'd be staying in that harsh land, they thought, to try to make some money.

He had come with them. There was nothing at the station but swarms of mosquitoes, which attacked them, and a waiting bus. They got in and it pulled out and the taiga looked on. Ahead was a truck loaded with logs, their pointed ends protruding from the back, gently swaying to the rhythm of the rutted road. Then, where the road took a slight turn, the truck veered and crashed into the trees on the other side. The bus tried to avoid it but failed, and impaled itself on the stack of sharpened logs.

Now, crouching with his beard resting on his knees, Vasil gazed into the fire and reflected on how lucky he had been. He could easily have been one of them. Skewered on the giant spits, and hanging in the air. Bloodied and moaning, or dead. But he wasn't. Death had passed him by, leaving just the salty taste of blood in his mouth. He shivered in horror, revulsion and pleasure. The pleasure of having survived, of having remained alive, if spattered with other people's blood.

Months had passed since the accident, but he still felt the shivers in his spine whenever he thought about it. Normally he would think about something else.

About her and about the child. As the days went by, he missed them more and more, a feeling made all the worse by the conditions he found himself living in. His desire to see them was powerful, but they were too far, thousands of miles away. But surely they thought about him from time to time? Well, he hoped so, and that they were expecting him to come back. Yes, of course, and when he did go back, everything would be as in the good old days.

He hadn't written to them about the accident. He'd wanted to, but hadn't. Better that they didn't know. They would only worry – besides, as he had escaped it didn't really matter. The point was that he had made it and things were working out, piece by piece. He'd always known that he would have a hard time, but still things were not quite what he had imagined. As a teacher, the toughest thing he'd had to do was hold a piece of chalk to the blackboard. But here the thing was to hold a shovel and spread concrete. His body had troubled him at first, with a tendency to go numb, but eventually it seemed to pick up the pace and now he thought he was coping rather well. He'd been with the same labour crew from the very start and had begun making good money from the second month. Other newcomers moved from team to team, slave-driven and then kicked out, but you had to keep your job for at least a month in order to get paid as much as the others.

He got on well with the other workers. At first they seemed rough and unfriendly, but he gradually got used to them, realizing they were all basically good, self-contained sorts, hardened by the work. They would toil away together, sometimes twelve or fourteen hours a day, especially in summer when the days were endless.

They were cutting a road through the taiga. The surface they laid was concrete so as not to crack in the winter cold. The road progressed, but so did the seasons. The ground was already frozen. No snow had yet fallen, but it could start any time, and it would be much harder work then. That's why the bosses were in such a rush, eager to stay on schedule. The foreman had put the screws on them. He said that if they just kept working at the same rate he'd cut their bonus. Haggard and skinny, he'd stand there at the worksite in his leather boots and black jacket, hands in pockets, smoking and watching them with his mousy eyes. Sometimes he'd come up behind them, snort hard and then hack up a phlegmy gobbet onto the still wet concrete, treat them to a sour look and then, without saying a word, get back in the jeep.

They didn't like him either. He was always threatening that one day he'd fire them and send them back on the happy train. That's what they called it, the train for people who had broken the law here, or committed some breach of discipline or other that got them sacked. They were sent back to Bulgaria: criminals to be tried, the others to pay damages which were often pretty steep. So they tried to lie low and not argue with him too much, since he was a creature of the Big Boss, and *he* would sign a dismissal without batting an eyelid.

They were expected to get as far as the river by the end of the year, but that was some distance through the taiga. Then again, there were problems with the deliveries of concrete. Your hands were tied. You just had to sit back and wait for the dump trucks to turn up. In summer you could lie back on a plank and doze off, but in the winter you couldn't do much more than hang around in the freezing cold. Sometimes a fire would be lit. Roasting skewered mushrooms might accompany a game of cards and some unlikely stories. Doing nothing jaded them as much as the work itself, even though everyone needed a break from time to time. When the trucks came back, loaded with concrete, the foreman would turn up and rush towards them, all agitated: 'Back to work! You've gone as mushy as roast leek!' He threw his weight around but actually he got paid little more than the rest of them. The big money stayed with the big bosses. They stole it. They forced the workers to keep doing overtime, but never paid them for it. Even on Sundays.

Holidays were made up for by working weekends. Sometimes they'd slave away for two or three weeks without a break and still get the same pay. Everyone wanted to rest; they needed some drinking time, they didn't feel like working. And they couldn't give a damn about the work schedule; it was all the same to them whether they reached the river or hell fire. Today they had said they wouldn't go to work, but in the end they did, the same as always, cussing and swearing. There was no point in needless conflict; the bosses had got their number anyway. If they didn't go they'd only get into deeper trouble, without really changing anything. They'd just be told to fuck off and then lose their bonus money. If they gave in and did it for appearance's sake it would be much better, so they went to work this Sunday to steer clear of trouble.

Vasil was the only one to stay in the hut. The others would tell the foreman that he had heart trouble. It was true, lately his heart had started hurting – the occasional pang, but nothing he took that seriously. It came and went, nothing really, nothing he couldn't live with. All he had to do was relax for a minute and take a deep breath, and the pain would go. It had happened once at work, but he'd quickly recovered. They had left him in the hut to chop wood so that in the holidays they could have logs for the fire.

He got down to work as soon as they left. He cut several logs with the chain saw, shaping them into blocks, neither too long nor too short – just the right size for the force of his blow as he struck with the axe. Splitting each block, first in two and then in four, he arranged them in piles along the back wall of the hut. The job took time but he enjoyed doing it. He liked seeing the blade of the axe split the timber, driven in by his own strength, and after each blow he was heady with a sense of his own physical power and skill.

He took some of the logs into the hut and arranged them in the hearth, which they had cast from concrete to avoid setting the wooden walls on fire. This hearth was hot enough, and an improvement on the stoves which had been provided originally. Made from tin, they cooled fast, while the cement absorbed the heat and stayed warm till dawn.

He arranged the logs in the centre of the hearth, pushing in and lighting some kindling at the bottom. The hut was small and heated up fast. Only Yaskata and he lived in it. They got along fine together, even though Yaskata was something of a square peg in a round hole. He was a heavy drinker (but then, who wasn't?) who seldom said anything. Occasionally he'd crack a joke, but more often just smile. Everything Vasil knew about him he'd learnt from the others. He was told that Yaskata had been married twice, but his first marriage hadn't worked out and his wife had left him and their two kids. Later, he had tried again and married another woman, but the money he made was barely enough to support the kids. So he'd come here, to earn enough both for his second wife and his kids. Soon after his arrival, he had asked his wife to join him, since newly wed women shouldn't be left alone. And she'd come and lived with him and hung around for a while, until one day she left. Vasil had no idea if her husband had sent her back or if she'd decided to go herself. There were various rumours about her in camp, more or less sinful stories, but he never learnt the truth.

One thing was beyond doubt: this was no place for women, and for married women in particular. Yet there were some, and these women were known to earn (so to speak) considerably more than their husbands, but they were few and far between. Single women were officially forbidden to be there, but Russian ones were there anyway. Whole trainloads of whores streamed in from all over the country. They usually came at the end of the month, around payday. Swarming all over the camps, they knocked on doors and windows, exposing a breast here, a thigh there, to show the tattooed fees for their services. After each customer, they squeezed a quick vinegar sponge between their legs and moved on to the next one. Vasil always declined their offers, although many were insistent or even aggressive. He didn't feel up to it, disgusted, so he went out, crossed the camp and withdrew into the forest.

There weren't many other huts like theirs. Most men lived in ancient, long defunct locomotives and carriages, strung along a sort of abandoned blind track. Washed up by the stream of time, the carriages stood here, in this god-forsaken place, huddled together and lost in remembrance, no doubt, of their glorious youth, when they had been involved full steam in History, transporting Humanity towards the future. For its part, Humanity, having travelled as far as it wished to go, had hurried to discard the loyal but clumsy steam engines, stranding them here as if afraid that someone might find them and contrive to navigate a reverse journey. Yet in time a use had been found for them, and although those who now possessed them had no ultimate destination in prospect, they engineered a little comfort. As these

historical monuments were nothing but a heap of scrap
barely suitable for shelter, the camp was known as Scrap
Town. Living in the cars was not regarded as something
to be coveted, so Vasil had been relatively fortunate to be
put up in one of the few nearby huts. Before his arrival,
Yaskata had lived there with his wife, and after she left
the bed had remained vacant, so Vasil moved in.
Sometimes odds and ends would pop up: clasps,
hairpins, indeed hair, which very tangibly bespoke her
recent presence in the room. Yaskata did not seem to
notice. Usually he would take any opportunity to fill
himself up with vodka and fall asleep.

The hut had the advantage of being next to the
train-house, so the others always came over to their
place. They usually drank and played cards, whereas he
himself did neither. It got on his nerves and, at least to
begin with, he couldn't get enough sleep. Gradually he
adapted and acquired the knack of sleeping even when
it was noisy, but it was better when there was nobody
and no noise except some vague rumbling in the cars,
and he could get a good rest.

There wasn't much furniture in the room, just the
bare essentials: a table, cupboard and two beds. On the
wall between them was a gun that Yaskata had bought in
the black market, ages ago. They seldom used it, so it just
hung there on a nail, just in case. You never knew what
you would need here, the back of beyond. Occasionally in
the taiga they ran into bear or elk, which they would kill
and then divide up the meat. Earlier in the year they had

shot a she-bear and three cubs. Apparently something had scared her, since she showed up in Scrap Town just as the men were about to go to work. Everyone pulled out their guns and started shooting. The heavy animal collapsed to the ground, ripped through by countless shots, and the cubs – still sucklings – growled and rubbed their snouts against their mother's body. They pulled them away and hacked up their mother, that they roasted the same night, then they fed the cubs until they were plump enough for slaughter too.

He had done all he had to do, so he sat for a while to warm up by the fire until the others came back. He was expecting them any minute, but he was hoping they would be a bit late, he didn't feel like budging and he enjoyed the solitude. The fire flicked out its scathing tongues at him. He took a log and cast it into the hearth. He saw how the raw wood flared up, oozing out resin with a hiss, drenching the air with its aroma. The smell crept up his nostrils and percolated through his lungs, reminding him of a picnic in the woods.

It had been the three of them – Vasil and her and the boy. Dusk was falling; the sun had just set behind the mountain ridge. They gathered twigs and lit a fire. There was this very same smell of burnt pine resin. They lay back, gazing at the slowly sailing red clouds. He hugged his wife and kissed her. 'I'll go and get more wood,' the child said. Then they heard the bump and the fall. He had walked straight into the trunk of one of the pine trees. As a toddler he was always tripping over things, but they'd thought it was just clumsiness and that he'd probably grow out of it. But it proved to be something else. He was losing his sight.

The revelation turned everything upside down. At first, Vasil just couldn't accept this; it had to be some sort of mistake. But gradually he came to understand that it was true and that he had to deal with it. As soon as he'd recovered from the initial shock, he tried to find out what practical things could be done. The different doctors he spoke to each put on a show of reassurance, impatient to get rid of him as quickly as possible. He tried to consult a professor recommended as the authority in the field. Getting an appointment proved very difficult, but eventually he managed to find someone who could arrange it. He took his son there as soon as he could. During the examination, the professor did not say a word. When he had finished, he reclined in his armchair, deep in thought, and his face showing nothing – or at least nothing that had to do with the examination. Sitting like this for a while, he said 'Mario needs surgery, but there's no one to do it.' At the time Vasil didn't understand what the professor meant by that 'no one to do it', but he soon realized. None of the few experts who were competent to operate on the boy were prepared to. They said that yes, he *could* be hospitalised in the Odessa ophthalmological clinic, but explained regretfully that no, it was not a straightforward matter, and, alas, there were bound to be long delays. Yet the examinations showed that the condition of the child was deteriorating and the operation should take place as soon as possible.

They decided to use their own devices. Just the child and him. When the ship sailed away, he could see his wife weeping on the quayside. After that, she would often weep – trying to hide her tears from the child when he was there, but otherwise, especially at night, crying and crying without restraint. She was overwrought, said nothing and easily fell into a fit of depression. When he tried to reassure her, she turned her back on him and went somewhere to be alone. He felt slighted and rejected, but at the same time tried to understand her and couldn't hold her to blame. He hoped that everything would be all right once Mario was cured. The boy was too young and did not understand exactly what was going on, but obviously knew something was wrong. He would goggle at them and uncharacteristically not ask any questions, just nodding obediently when they told him to be good when he was being examined. He was just as silent on board the ship, but as they sat on the deck watching the waves he suddenly asked, 'Daddy, what's on the bottom of the sea?'

In Odessa, he was able to contact the doctor with little difficulty. The expert received them in his consulting room and studied the boy's epicrisis. 'He's going to be fine,' he announced finally. Something about the way he spoke inspired trust. 'But I'll want 5,000 roubles,' he added. 'In cash.'

Vasil hadn't told the others why he had come. The only reason anyone came here was because they were in a bad way and they hoped that by making some money the problems could be fixed and they'd be able to piece things together. True, they did make good money, two or three times what they'd make back home; and then, there was nothing to spend it on in this wasteland, which should have helped. But the fact was that eventually people broke down and started drinking too much without realizing it. Alcohol replaced the blood flowing in their veins, sapped their strength and forced them to work just in order to have something to drink at night. Very soon, a single night would be insufficient to quench their thirst. So it went on. They would drink for nights, weeks, months, years on end, until they had no savings and no clothes to sell, and ultimately turned into shrivelled skeletons covered with chapped skin. Then they were bundled onto the happy train and sent back to their families, if they still had any.

Not everyone hit the bottle. Some resisted alcohol, made good money and when their contract expired, left, but only to come back again soon. Like the prisoner who had said to him: 'All my best mates are in jail, so what am I going to do outside?'

He knew the others had their own problems, too, though they didn't show it and tried to appear indifferent. He often saw a group of them standing in between the steel carriages. They pretended to be pissing, but really they were struggling to make sense of their problems until, giving up, they just bashed their heads against the rusty iron instead. He pretended he hadn't seen them and hurried on because he didn't want to intrude on their thoughts. They were black, spattered thoughts. That's why they hid them deep down inside. If they were to own up, those dark, heavy thoughts would become all the darker and heavier, so each one of them instinctively clenched his teeth and stayed silent. This silence accumulated and spread wide across Scrap Town, acquiring ever-greater mass, and each word that was uttered resounded within this void of silence. At times he, too, felt like screaming his pain out, but even if he had done it nothing would have changed, so he did what everybody else did. He held his tongue.

The thoughts had tired him. He felt his head heavy and his body tired. He rested on his elbows and slumped on the floor. His eyes moved across the ceiling, as the spreading warmth stirred the cockroaches up there. They were content, it seemed. So was he, content to watch them scuttle about with their few cares; he felt an affinity with them, for they were the only creatures, apart from men, who had dared crawl that far north. He called out to them in his sleep, and they came, encircled him and started dancing in a chain. Although he couldn't hear any music, they swayed to a secret rhythm, the circle gradually closed in and then they were almost in his face... He smelt bad breath and opened his eyes to see a panting dog. The animal gazed at him with its yellow eyes which reflected his own. Sava was holding it, a stout fellow with a big black moustache and long straight hair spilling down his back. His heavy hand gripped thick whipcord wound around the dog's powerful neck.

'You sleeping?' the man laughed.

'What's that?'

'Eskimo dog. It came by itself. Popped up on the road and followed our tracks.'

Obviously he had fallen asleep – a deep sleep, since he hadn't heard them come in. It must have been a while ago, since there was Yaskata warming himself by the fire, his old worn cotton jacket draped on his shoulders, and the light from the flames dancing on his bare chest. He was well-built but somehow looked short and skinny, his face drawn – almost delicate – and sparsely bearded, while his left eye constantly squinted because of an old frozen wound, as a result of which you couldn't see the eye very well. Cross-legged, he stroked the polished shaft of the axe. But what on earth was that dog doing inside? Sava was still holding it over him, and it went on panting in his face, mouth open and tongue lolling. It had thick coarse hair and a black whorl across the chest, which extended up the stout neck and muzzle to the forehead. The dog sniffed him, nodded and gently licked his cheek.

He raised his arm to stroke the dog's neck. A beautiful thing, a creature of the North. It reminded him of that day when he had gone into the forest and the taiga had swallowed him. He was gathering mushrooms, and when he had gathered enough he decided to go back. On and on he walked, the camp nowhere in sight, just trees everywhere, endless, trunks towering up to the sky. He quickened his pace and became breathless, then found he was wading into a swamp and reversed his steps. He saw that built on firmer ground was a small hut. When he pushed aside its reed door, a gun barrel was pointing at his face, and behind it he had a momentary impression of someone hairy and humpbacked and snarling. Instantly he fled, and just kept running, regardless of the direction, until eventually he tripped and fell. There was something growling like a wolf. He raised his head from the wet moss and saw it was an Eskimo dog.

As he looked around he saw the rest of them, a whole pack of dogs gone wild. He raised his exhausted body, soaked in cold sweat, and backed away. And he never took his eyes off the dogs, which were constantly growling and bristling, as he retreated. After a long time, he heard human voices behind him. He risked a glance over his shoulder and realized he was back in the camp. The dogs had guided him there. Much later, he learned that the creature in the hut was a harmless old cripple who had forgotten how to speak. He had fled to the taiga during the war and remained there ever since, hidden and alone, staying alive on such game and fish as he managed to catch, wholly unaware that the fighting had ended decades before.

'C'mon,' Sava urged, and led the dog outside. The creature obeyed, walking confidently after him, its powerful back gracefully arched and its raised, bushy tail wagging. Yaskata had followed.

Through the open door he saw Yaskata raise the axe and then crash it down on the head of the dog. He hit it with the blunt side, cracking the skull. It briefly whined, dug its claws into the ground, tensed its muscles and arched its back; then collapsed. Sava bent down and slipped the cord from the dog's neck, clasped the hind legs and bound them together. Then he lifted the dead beast and hung it on a broken-down hoist behind him, which could have been designed for the very purpose. He reached inside his jacket and produced a knife. The dog, hanging there like that, with teeth bared and eyes glazed, looked very different from its appearance when alive. It was now much larger, and sinister.

Vasil felt sick. He had eaten dog before, occasionally, but had never seen one butchered. Something stirred in his stomach, swelled up and then stopped in his throat. He slowly rose to his feet and went outside, in no great hurry, as he didn't want the others to know. Once behind the hut he threw up, and he felt a sense of relief. He took a deep breath of fresh air and wiped his sleeve across his eyes to dry them, and then looked up. The sky was very close, and clouds were sailing along it to infinity.

When he looked down again, a pair of child's eyes – big and blue – were watching him, full of fear. He had seen them before. They belonged to Lida's daughter. The mother regularly hawked herself around, and by turns she'd get vodka, abuse and a beating, before being thrown out along with the child who accompanied her. Then she'd knock on another door and it would happen all over again. Some days, when the men were away at work, she tried to clean up, light the fire or stove and wait for them in the warm. But when they were drunk and their money had run out or they'd simply had enough of her, they told her to go to hell. Then you might find her sprawled out somewhere, probably stark naked, alone but for a sobbing little girl. Sometimes the police locked her up for a few nights, but soon released her and it was back to the usual. The other whores didn't stick around the camp for long, but Lida never left.

It was said she'd been a drama student in Moscow, where she met a Bulgarian. They married and went to live in his country. Then he had to go to Africa on business, and when he came back he found out what she'd been up to in his absence. After the divorce she married someone else, and when he signed up for work at Komi she went with him. But again, whether because of her generous nature or pressure of circumstances, her second husband left her for much the same reasons as his predecessor. She stayed on though, and after a certain time produced a baby girl. No one knew who the father was, least of all Lida. The child shared all the horrible experiences of the mother. She almost froze to death with her. Or starved. Sometimes she shared a beating.

Now she just stood there and watched him with apparent indifference. She was almost his son's age. Dirty matted locks of mousy blonde hair fell across a small round face stained with ink pencil. There were traces of old varnish on her little fingernails. The scruffy blue coat and oversize, nearly matching boots she wore didn't stop her shivering. He had an urge to take her in his arms, hold her tightly to his heart and then lead her away from this awful place. He held out his hand. The little girl stared at it, then turned and ran off.

In front of the hut, he saw that Sava had finished flaying the dog and was now busy gutting it. He dumped the entrails straight on the frozen ground, which melted a bit from the warmth of the blood. But soon it was all frozen again. Crows had descended on the nearby trees and were raucously staking their claims.

The men often fed on dogs, if there were any. Especially on holidays: they roasted them like lamb on St George's Day. The usual meat they got was stamped from 1947 and didn't smell too good. If you ate it, you got a stomachache. But if you're doing hard work, you can't just live on beans, rice and potatoes – you'd become anaemic. No, you need some sort of meat. Besides, it goes with alcohol.

So when anyone drove to the village, they'd try to nab a stray Maltese terrier. You'd find lots of them there, poking around in the garbage. Easy to catch, and said by the discerning to yield tenderer meat than the Eskimo dogs, if in lesser quantity. There were no dogs in the camp, except for the Maltese that Meto had. He watched over her with all the vigilance a parent might exercise on a child. But one day she was bound to disappear too, with nothing but bones left. Perhaps there was nothing wrong in eating these animals. It had a certain, as one might say, pedigree. The ancient Bulgarians were said to have slaughtered dogs on sacred days and drunk the blood, while the ancient Greeks sacrificed them at crossroads, to propitiate the goddess Hecate. This dog might have been very old – as old as life itself – and reincarnated, brought into this world by men's hunger. Still, you couldn't help thinking there was something rather nasty about the whole business.

As he walked past Sava, he saw him still industriously ferreting and filleting away. With his sinewy build and his long hair combed back, he looked like an aristocratic oriental from a bygone age. Vasil went inside, leaving the door open to let in the light and air. Yaskata was in his usual place by the hearth. He often sat there like that, gazing into the fire and lost in silent thought. Sometimes at night, just before dozing off, Vasil would be aware of him sitting with a bottle of vodka in his lap, grunting a bit now and then. Then when he woke up for work the next morning, he'd see Yaskata still in exactly the same position, sitting cross-legged by the long-dead fire with a now empty bottle.

'That was a good whack you gave that dog,' he told him, to break the silence. 'Very neat.' He thought

Yaskata would confine a reply to his usual silent nod. But this time the other man started talking.

'It's my job.'

He glanced through the door at Sava, still busy with the dog, before continuing.

'When I was a boy there were poplars near our place. Old, big ones. Lots of birds nested in them. One day they decided to widen the street and cut them down. Most of the baby birds had just hatched, and when the trees came crashing down, you heard this squealing, from all these little birds. The parents were just fluttering about, couldn't do anything. So I took as many of the babies home as I could, made some cages and started feeding them. There were different sorts, Sparrows, blackbirds, starlings, turtledoves – even nightingales. I had other pets at home, too. Two dogs, a cat, some tortoises, and jars full of field mice. They took up most of my time, so I skipped school quite often. It was the baby birds that needed a lot of extra seeing-to, though. Some of them had to have maggots to eat, so I used to collect them from under tree bark. Then of course I had to feed them one by one, so it took quite a long time. I stopped going to school. The teachers started calling in at home but I didn't want to tell them anything. They threatened I'd be expelled, and that's what happened. So I got sent to a reformatory, and the work they made you do there was called *reformative labour*. In my case they thought it would be good if I worked in a slaughterhouse. Killing animals…'

He thought Yaskata was crying. But as he looked more closely at his friend's one good, deep-set eye he decided he was mistaken. It was a trick of the light that made it look sad and tearful.

'Cheer up!' Sava called out. Resting against the doorframe, he almost filled the entrance. He strode past them, and drove the bloodstained knife into the table. 'It'll soon be the holiday.'

Meaning the Ninth of September, which was in Bulgaria the celebration of the glorious Victory of the People over the dark forces of capitalism and fascism.

'Fuck that,' Yaskata replied. 'But where's that bloke with the booze?'

Usually Gocheto would take the truck and drive down to the village to get fresh supplies of alcohol. But on the eve of the holidays, the usual place was sold out and you had to go to Old Igor. He was a war veteran who, though he still lived in a dump, was said to have made millions from bootlegging vodka over the years. Gocheto seemed to have hit it off with him, and got the stuff at a special discount. This time he was late, though. He never returned empty-handed, but he might well have consumed a sizeable amount of his purchase before starting to drive back.

'He'll be back all right,' Sava declared, as he picked up a greasy iron bar from the corner of the room. 'That dog's too big for the hearth. We'll have to roast it in the open instead of stewing it.'

'So what?'

So what indeed, it would be tougher, but that didn't really matter. It was meat, wasn't it – fresh meat, at that. At least they wouldn't drink on an empty stomach. He decided to stretch his legs. He left Yaskata deep in thought by the hearth, and stepped outside. A slight but chilling wind was blowing. He took an armful of logs and dumped them a few metres in front of the hut. Dowsing them in machine oil, he set the logs on fire. Sava came along with the long iron spit. He skewered the dog and left it hanging on a hook. Then he brought two equally tall blocks and arranged them by the fire, took the dog off the hook and balanced it on them, near the strong flames. The searing tongues of fire caressed the flayed animal.

'Needs lots of turning,' Sava declared.

'Be ready by tomorrow.'

'Sure.'

The camp had livened up, and the old train looked as if it might let off steam and pull out any moment, waiting only for the signal. The men were coming back from work and preparing to rest. They popped in and out in haste, as if afraid that the others would leave without them. They quickly washed, stripped to the waist, pouring buckets of cold water over each other, and then shaved. To check what was happening, they poked their lathered heads out from the open windows of the cars, before changing from their soiled working clothes into clean ones. Some simply sat on the iron steps of the cars, legs dangling down sipping drinks.

The clatter and smoke of lit stoves blended with the odour of male bodies and soapy water, permeating Scrap Town. Some were about to go and visit friends in the neighbouring village. Others stayed on. They simply had nowhere to go.

Sava had settled down comfortably on a stump near the fire and was working on his embroidery, keeping one eye on the spitted dog. He did not use an embroidery frame, and the needle was lost in his swollen meaty fingers. He was careful with each stitch, gently pulling the thread through. Though this was unusual for a man of such Herculean build and with labourer's hands like his, he did it with great application and duly produced magnificent tapestries, embroidered with patience and love. Once a tapestry was finished, he would hang it on his wall and feast his eyes on it for a few days. After which he gave it away to friends, or he left it by a stump in the taiga. 'That's for the taiga,' he would say.

Vasil peeked over his shoulder, trying to get a good look at the embroidery. Although the canvas was crumpled and gathered together in its maker's hands, the figures were easy to make out. Two children, one dark and one fair, were leaning over the brink of a precipice, a hair's breadth away from death, but up against a grey sky, white wings outspread, a guardian angel watched over them. The tapestry seemed almost ready, since the composition was complete, and only some orange clouds in the sky had to be filled in.

'Ready soon?'

'It's done,' Sava replied without looking up, absorbed in his work.

Meto's Maltese terrier ran out of the hut nearby, followed by Meto. The terrier paused by a pine-tree, crouched thoughtfully and urinated. The dog had belonged to a whore who had lived with Meto for a while but then left, leaving him to care for the dog.

Meto was skinny, with a long face and veined arms. He was in a sour mood most of the time, and spoke to no one but his dog. After him came his roommate, Hesho the Gypsy, with a small knitted cap on his head, a cap he never took off since he had lost his hair. It happened the moment he set foot in Komi; the doctors told him it was caused by the magnetic storms prevalent in the region, which was why he was paid danger money. His lack of hair made his Gypsy features less obvious, but the dark skin and pale yellow eyeballs gave away his ancestry (which he strenuously denied). Neither were too friendly – lone wolves, really – and they kept a low profile, although the two of them were known to have fallen out often. As soon as they saw the others sitting by the fire, they came up and stared at the spitted dog.

'Gonna eat it?' Meto asked.

'Yes, then we're gonna roast yours,' Sava replied.

The Maltese was running around, heedless of her cousin's fate. Her master bent down, lifted her and carried her into the hut. He locked her inside, after bringing out his fishing rod. Then he padlocked the door.

'Beat it – lost heart and beat it,' Hesho grinned. 'Might go to bed with it one day, for all you know,' he added with a knowing look. They were at daggers over the dog. Meto kept her locked indoors because he knew that left alone outdoors she would disappear. On the other hand, Hesho complained that she chewed his shoes and dribbled all over them, slept on his suitcase and rummaged in his things. You could often hear them quarrelling, and they would finally go to bed with no solution found.

'Off to fish now. That dog's like a cat – eats fish – and he catches fish and brings it back for her,' Hesho explained. 'He almost got shot doing it once.'

Near the River Mezen there was sometimes shooting between salmon poachers and bailiffs. These two tribes usually avoided each other, but when they did meet, loss of life often resulted.

One night Meto had been crouching on the bank, catching crucian carp for his dog, when the bailiffs opened fire. A stray bullet caught him in the hand, and he came back to camp bleeding and shaking. That was a few months before and everyone knew about it, but Hesho obviously felt he knew something more. Now he lingered on, musing and clicking his tongue. He loitered around the fire and looked the dog over.

'That's a fine dog. Where d'you find it?' he inquired.

Intent on his tapestry, Sava seemed not to have heard him and painstakingly went on embroidering.

'But it'll be tough,' continued Hesho, with increasing interest in the dog. 'Might be sour, too.'

'Shut up, Hesho.' Sava, who apparently wasn't in the mood for Hesho's observations, cut him short.

'I'm going to get a drink,' Hesho announced, disgruntled, and hastened on to his hut, startling the crows that had crowded around the dumped entrails and were noisily squabbling over them. But in no time they had regathered and were pecking away again with even more gusto, their glittering black eyes glancing around warily all the while. Then suddenly they all flew away, and shortly afterwards a lorry roared to a stop. It was spattered with mud up to the windows. The door opened and out came Gocheto in a vest and a hat with earflaps drooping on both sides. He walked over to the other side and opened the door. There were two crates on the seat.

'Andropovka,' he explained.

'Couldn't find anything worse?' asked Yaskata, who had come out and was glaring at him.

'They've killed Old Igor. Shot him in the face. Blew his head off,' explained Gocheto, carrying the crates.

'Why?'

'Who knows? Could be the vodka, could be the cash – maybe both. They say it was the convicts.'

'What convicts?'

'Escaped from prison. In one of the neighbourhoods a little girl saw them. So they slit her throat. The father was there and went for them. So they slit his throat, too. Then they went into the house, killed the mother, took some provisions and ran away. A neighbour saw it all but stayed away.'

'Did well to.' Yaskata grinned, opened a bottle of brandy, took a swig and passed it on to the others.

Sometimes they found human skeletons in the forest. Picked clean, and mute. Perhaps none but time knew who they had belonged to. They were assumed to have been prisoners on the run. Having sought deliverance in the taiga, they were blessed by it with eternal peace. Ordinary men who did not know its laws could hardly survive in it. But in ignorance they would run away. Wild and frantic, spurred on by a thirst for freedom and life, in search of the path to salvation. In prison lurked death. All they got was scraps of food. Wasting away, they fell sick and died before their long terms were up. Some who were strong took the food intended for others, hoarded it and then one day headed for… freedom. It was waiting for them outside, out there, beautiful and alluring. It stretched out a hand and smiled coyly. It lured them on, and then it vanished, stranding them lonely and exhausted in the cold night that was closing upon them. Yet now, tender and transparent in its dawn, it engulfed them, warmed by their own fire, united by a flayed dog.

'Bet they don't know where they're going!' Sava interjected.

'Yes they do,' Yaskata countered.

'So I couldn't get anything from Old Igor,' Gocheto went on. 'I bought this from the assistant chef at the canteen for ten roubles more. We come from the same part of the country and he stocks up to have something for his mates. On my way out I took a look at the kitchen. There they were, making tomato salad, with two suckling pigs arranged in baking tins. Is that for dinner or breakfast? I wondered. Then I felt a hand on my shoulder. Turned round – it was the foreman. "What're you doing here?" he says. "Why weren't you at work?" So I told him I had been, but when we heard the pigs squeal we'd rushed to help because, you see, the poor things feared for their skins and might run away before you knew it, then who's gonna chase them in the woods? He stood there, breathing heavy with his big hairy nostrils. His hand grabbed me, like he was gonna skin me alive. Then he started screaming – frothing at the mouth, all over the place. "Get out of here!" he yelled, "Or your arse is going to be in big trouble. Pigs my arse, you lying git. You ain't going to see another pig in all your natural! Now fuck off!" he yelled, and pointed at the door.'

'If I were you I'd have hit him,' Sava said curtly in his deep gruff voice.

'It's not worth wasting time on that piece of shit,' Gocheto advised him.

'On the contrary, it *is* worth it. If only those jailbirds had nabbed him instead of those other poor bastards, they'd have atoned for their sins three times over.'

'Anyway, I thought it was too early for me to atone, so I got my arse out of there before I was in deep shit.'

'And right you were,' Yaskata backed him, opening another bottle instead of waiting for the others to pass the first one back.

'That's right. Only it can't go on this way. You can't have all the pains for some and all the gains for others. Fucking bastard, forcing me to work Sundays, threatening me with the law – "those who didn't report for work would be seen as enemies of the people" – bollocks! The cheek of it! He has the pig and you're an enemy of the people 'cos you upset his meal!'

'It can go on, it always does.'

The conversation went round with the bottle; occasionally it stopped, and then went on again, passing Vasil lightly, almost without touching him. He felt it grow hotter, condemning, hating, absorbing the warmth from the fire and flying on to infinity. The strong brandy burnt his throat, drowning him in the bitter memory of a pair of child's eyes. They gazed at him and cried for help. They appealed to him, beseeching and suffering, watched him innocently as blindness itself. The smoke made his eyes smart. They disobeyed him despite all his male willpower, and two small salty tears rolled partway down before being dried by the wind. He knelt there, bent over, clutching his sorrow in his belly. A man powerful yet impotent, borne by chaos and existing in it, crawling towards the next day like a caterpillar with no thought of butterflies, at best a cocoon.

The dog was roasting on the embers, stretched and red-hot. He peered at it and saw himself. Yes, it was his own face that stared back at him out of the white of the eye. Flushed and sweating with the heat, it seemed to be smirking. He felt the flames burn his belly as if something was cutting him in two. The pain became more and more unbearable, spreading across his body. Strangely enough, it seemed to come from inside him. He looked at his hands. They were holding an empty bottle. The taste of brandy lingered on in his mouth, while the dog hung there, spitted, with Sava carefully turning it from time to time. He could well have been in its place, like the others in the bus on the way here. Dog or man – what was the difference? An accident or a prejudice, perhaps?

He looked around, without moving from his place. That was good. Much better, at least for the time being. Night had caught up with them and he saw the shadows of the others gently swaying, along with his own, and chatting.

'Once I've made some real money you'll see what Gocheto can do with life,' boasted the voice. 'First I'll get myself a car. A blue one with white seats. I know what the good life is and I don't care if anyone else says it's vulgar. I'm not going to wait for ages on the application list. Slip 'em a bribe and they'll deliver right to the door. In I get and off to the lake, lazing around on the beach all day. Never any places for us, are there? Well, you just pull out a wad, even if there are no places. Once they see the cash, they'll sell their arse. Then wherever you go, they'll be licking their lips at you, dozens of those bitches all standing in line. I'll choose the fittest ones. A black one on one side and a blonde on the other, to just do whatever, and I'll shove bank notes down their tits. All those wankers'll be looking and getting it up. Let 'em get it up! That's all they're gonna get...'

Dreams. Big or silly or the simplest of human dreams. Simple, but yours. Faint or impossible ones that might be displaced by real hopes. He had hopes, too. He believed that one day he would go back. They would be together again, all three of them, forever. Healthy and happy, strolling by the river, the boy running ahead and skimming flat stones on the water's surface, and she gently smiling, embracing him. He could feel the soft touch of her hair on his cheek. How much he missed her. He had never known before how much he needed her and he had never desired her as strongly. He longed for her full lips, for the fragrance of her body and for her herself. 'Come back as soon as possible. We'll be expecting you!' She had told him on departure, adding with a gentle kiss: 'I love you.' At that point he had felt sorry. He felt as if he were to blame for something. He wanted to take both of them in his arms and clasp them in an eternal embrace, but all he managed to say was a formal 'Goodbye!' and then he got in the car to hide his emotions. What were she and the child doing now? So far away, without him. They hadn't written for ages. The last letter had come months ago. God knows why, but he had found it somewhat... curt. He might have imagined it, but the earlier ones seemed not only more frequent but kinder somehow. Then again, he didn't write much to her either. The important thing was for it all to be over and made good. He knew they were waiting for him and he had to go back.

'This party without females reminds me of when we had time off in the army. We used to sit in front of the TV in the political club. Then when someone appeared on the TV to make a speech, we turned the lights off, bent over, showed our bums to the TV and lit our farts. So we were *doing* something, at least. And what do we do now? Yackety-yack!' said Gocheto, indignant. He thought for a while and then smiled.

'Once they took us out from the barracks for 'cultural recreation' (as they liked to call it), and we found a poof,' he went on. 'In fact, he got what he wanted, the hairy-arsed old bastard. The next time he saw us, he ran a mile. I think he was still feeling a bit sore.'

'We can give you a try if you want to.'

'There used to be a work team here that fucked one of their men,' Sava broke in, 'But afterwards they collected enough money so they could buy him a big car. To say sorry, I suppose.'

The drinks had gone to their heads. Their blood started boiling. He didn't like them drunk, even when he was drunk himself. They became somehow distant and unreal, unless of course it was he himself who might have become unreal. A couple of months ago he and Sava were walking past the log trestles. All of a sudden there was a noise from the top of the pile that quickly became a roar, and he turned to see dozens of logs thundering down on them. Immediately Sava grabbed him with his powerful hands and shoved him aside, and jumped himself. The huge logs rolled past them like crazy giant steamrollers. This was real, and he could have ended up pulped under half a forest.

He felt the cold at the back of his neck. His group alone sat outdoors, keeping the tradition of the holidays. The few other people who had stayed on in camp were indoors in the warm. A door opened in one of the distant cars. A light came from inside, and two figures could be made out. One was shoved by the other. Then a third smaller figure appeared, following the first. Lida and the girl. She couldn't be having an easy time of it these days, Lida. In fact, she might well like to join them, unless someone stubbed his cigarette out on her rump, as had happened the previous holiday.

'My, my, here's whom we missed,' Gocheto exclaimed as soon as he saw them, rubbing his hands. 'Come here,' he called Lida.

She came up, stopped and looked around. She was wearing thick-soled shoes and an old red coat which, lacking buttons, she had to clasp together around her very possibly naked body. She stood there with her hair in a mess, collar pulled up.

'She looks a bit chilly. Give her a cigarette and a swig to warm up before we warm up ourselves,' Gocheto suggested with a grin, opening a bottle and pushing it into her hands.

She took it without a word, raised the bottle and swilled down half of it. The child stood in the shadow behind her, looking on timorously. She seemed to be hiding from somebody, perhaps them or the world in general. Yaskata fumbled in his pocket, took out a packet of cigarettes and, without turning round, offered them to the mother. She took one, lit it, inhaled deeply and let the smoke stream out through her nose. Then she leant on Yaskata's shoulder, smiled suggestively and ran her hand along his bare chest; but he jerked away, leapt to his feet and then pushed her so hard she fell onto the ground.

'Scram!' he yelled, with a fierce look.

'Aw, fuck off!' she swore and tried to get to her feet, while holding firmly on to the bottle. Gocheto grabbed her under the shoulders and lifted her drooping body.

'Come on princess, come with me, I love you. Leave him alone, there are other men. You know how good I am to you, don't you? So come on, calm down... come on...' Still cajoling her, Gocheto slowly led her off to the hut, guiding her by the hand.

'Watch out for Siberian syphilis,' Sava called out after him.

'If she brands me, I'll stuff a pig's tail up hers, bristles up!'

'You'll have to borrow it from the foreman!'

The little girl was about to follow them.

'Hey you, come here,' Vasil called out, and went to take her hand. She stopped in her tracks and stared at him suspiciously, then abruptly ran after her mother, crying out her name.

'She's used to it; it won't be the first time she's watched. Let her go,' Sava told him. He said it very calmly and with authority. He was the oldest of them all, had worked there for ten years, and ought to know what he was talking about.

This left the three of them outside. They sat in silence. The laughter that came from the hut gradually died down. Vasil thought of the little girl. What was she doing there? She must be sitting meekly on the other bed, looking on. She was waiting for them to be over and done with it. Maybe she was so used to it that she saw her mother's legs around some male body as a commonplace gesture of attention; perhaps she took the world in more or less as it was, refracted in the light of her child's eyes. But how were things refracted in a child's dreams?

One night, when they were making love under the bed cover, relaxed in the peace of the night, they heard Mario sobbing through the wall. 'Mummy, Mummy,' his voice echoed, chilling the passion in their bodies. The door opened, and he ran up, eyes wide open and brimming, squeezed between them and broke into tears. 'I'm scared,' he sobbed.

'What's the matter darling?'

'There's someone over there.'

'Don't be afraid. There's no one there. We're here and we're watching over you,' she soothed him with a motherly hug.

'But that woman was there in my room.'

'Which woman?'

'The woman in blue. She was in a blue dress; she was fat, with bare feet and grey hair. She came up with her back to me, and she had a big hump. She wanted to take me away, mummy. But I cried out and she started laughing and went away. I saw her go through the door.'

'Don't be afraid, love. It was all a dream. There's nothing to worry about. No one's come in or out. You had a bad dream, that's all. Come on, calm down now and go back to bed.'

'Don't want to. I'm scared.'

'Come on.'

'Okay, but if she comes back will daddy throw her out?'

'Certainly I will. Just let her come!' his father had said, pretending to be furious.

'Night daddy. Night mummy. I'm no chicken,' the little boy affirmed, wiping the tears from his eyes.

'Of course you aren't,' she replied with a kiss on his forehead. His father saw the small pink feet taking him back to his room, and the two of them, alone together again, looked at each other in fear, like terrified children. It was a strange thing. He had everything a child needed – domestic comfort, care and attention, and lots of toys; he was growing up in the best conditions they could provide. He had a room of his own, always nice and cosy, full of teddy bears and fairy tales, but still he had nightmares, and often. Sometimes he did not wake up, other times he would get up and hide in their bed, chased by his dream, by the shadows of creatures refracted in the light of his eyes, coming from a bright child's world before the curtain of darkness slowly falls, leaving only shadows.

What distorted visions would this little girl see in her dreams, a tiny flower in the slime, wilting from the stench, mindlessly conceived in animal wretchedness?

He thought he saw the Moon. He remembered very well how it had looked the night Mario was born. Large and healthy, with a pale golden halo. He was gazing at it and waiting for the baby to be born, to hear his voice. His wife was screaming. He could hear her screams distinctly, very close. He felt as if they came from him but knew they were hers and came from the room up there with a light in the window. He knew she was there, biting her lips, legs spread apart in anguish, moaning with pain, while the child pushed forward, wrapped in placenta, struggling to tear its way out to the world with its head and to shatter the silence of the night with infant cries. Alone with the Moon, he was waiting for the voice of life, while the Moon watched on benevolently from above, lending him patience and courage. That night outside the white building had been a long one. He sat in front of the shadows of trees and prayed to the Moon for help, to pull the child out as it pulled the tides of the sea, and that was when he heard the cry and realized that his son had been born. He looked up again to find the friendly Moon, but it was gone. He tried to locate it, wherever else in the firmament it might have moved, but only the stars shone up there. Close and remote, and invisible, they glittered down on him, flashing their rays of pure white magic. Infinite and eternal, they transmitted their inscrutable signals, mysteriously flickering like a multitude of tiny torches. Something hooted in the forest, some owl or other bird of the night.

Sava went over to Yskata 'What's wrong with you? What's on your mind?' he asked his friend. It was an unspoken thing between them. The two of them had the greatest authority in the team and without needing to speak to each other, they were invariably in agreement, established by time and a natural sympathy. Yaskata did not reply, he had lit a cigarette and was smoking. He inhaled the smoke deeply, held it in his lungs, and the embers of the cigarette made fast progress. Little by little, he turned his head to Sava and threw the butt in the fire.

'Best regards, to you and the boys.'

'From whom?'

'My wife.'

Sava said nothing. He glanced at him without a word.

'She wants a divorce,' Yaskata went on. 'Shall I give it to her?'

'You know best.'

'I do?'

A mechanical roar shattered the air. The door of the adjacent hut had burst open, and out ran Hesho, stark naked. Meto, who was brandishing a chain saw above his head, closely pursued him.

'I'm going to carve you into fucking pieces!' he seemed to be screaming, though the noise of the machine drowned everything else. Immediately Sava leapt to his feet, caught up with the madman and grabbed his wrists, shaking Meto's arms until the chain saw was dropped. Sava hurled it aside and pressed Meto to the ground, even though he showed no desire to fight back, lying motionless rather with a helpless look on his face. Everyone rushed to the scene; even Gocheto came out, half-naked, to see what was the matter. Only Hesho stayed at a cautious distance, shivering. After he decided that Meto was now pacified, Sava released him and, subdued now, he stood up unsteadily and staggered to the hut. He re-emerged hugging the Maltese terrier, which had been hiding under the bed. Then he carefully raised the tail, exposing to the general view the creature's pulsating sphincter.

'Look! Look at that!' he sobbed, and tears rolled down his cheeks. 'I've raised her, watched over her like a child, and then he goes and rapes her.' They stood there, looking at the canine anus and sharing Meto's grief.

'It's okay, Meto,' Gocheto tried to comfort him. 'You sure?'

'Of course, I saw him as soon as I opened the door!' he wailed, breaking into tears. 'My poor dog! What have they done to you, my poor darling?' he sobbed, hugging the animal – whose eyes, half-hidden by its forelocks, seemed to display an expression of some guilt.

'Stop it! Stop it. Meto, please do. Give yourself a break. Come on!' Sava urged him, gently steering him back to his bed. He did as he was told, eventually curling up in bed with the dog settled on his lap. He was still weeping as they left him and returned to the fire outside. Hesho slowly approached the group. He appeared uncomfortable, as a naked man would be on a night like that.

'You bastard,' Sava rebuked him, with clear distaste. 'How could you do it with a dog?'

'I couldn't help it. I was a bit pissed and I started feeling horny,' Hesho explained. 'Then all of a sudden there was this dog licking my hand. So I could tell what it wanted, obviously. So I just lifted it up and... you know...'

'But why didn't you do it with Lida instead of a dog?'

'I'm sick and tired of her, I can't even *feel* her anymore. And besides, she doesn't do anything, she just lies there and waits for it. But I'm a Gypsy – I've been used to animals since I was a boy, and they're used to me,' he muttered defensively. Naked and shivering, he looked pretty miserable.

'Was she a virgin?' Gocheto tittered.

'Go to our hut, it's warm in there,' Yaskata broke in.

Hesho didn't have to be asked twice. He turned round and went off, his bare backside conspicuously white in the darkness.

'I'm going to burn you all down!' Meto suddenly screamed. He had stormed out again, this time armed with flaming torches. He threw one at his hut and the other at theirs. They leapt up, rushed toward the buildings and managed to extinguish the flames before they reached the roofs.

'I'll set you on fire! I'll set everything on fire!' Meto went on screaming, waving his arms and kicking anyone who dared come close.

'Let's tie him up!' cried Gocheto, still half-naked and gripping the rope with which the dog had been tied earlier. Someone managed to trip Meto up, and then they pinned him down while his arms were tied. Though bound hand and foot, he kept squirming like a severed worm.

'He's cracked up,' Gocheto said.

'All for the sake of some mangy dog. I should've eaten it,' Hesho added behind them.

'You shut up,' Sava cut him short.

They stood there in a bunch, studying the man on the ground.

'Let's take him in so that we can keep an eye on him,' Gocheto suggested.

'Let's do that. We can play cards, too.'

'Sure, if someone stays outside to keep an eye on the dog.'

'I will,' Vasil volunteered. He didn't feel like going indoors anyway. He wanted to be by himself. He needed it.

'You'll never put the fire out! You'll all burn to ashes!' Meto's voice echoed across Scrap Town as they dragged him inside along with the crate of brandy.

Vasil turned back to the fire before him.

Fire, he thought, the possession of the gods. And given to mortals by a titan horribly punished by those gods for his transgression. Prometheus had suffered for what he, no doubt, believed to be a noble deed. But perhaps it was an unlucky one, and not only for him? Perhaps the gods' fury was well founded? Perhaps they were right: this was a supernatural force that they alone should possess. They knew (being gods) that mortals were petty and selfish creatures with little thought of whatever lay beyond their own demise. In their craving for power and glory in one short lifetime, they might destroy the very Earth in one exultant conflagration. And while this element, which he himself had kindled into life, lay amicably at his feet, warming him nice and cosily, he observed a tiny fly summarily gobbled up by the flames of what was, for the fly, a furnace. Such were Vasil's meditations.

The dog needed to be turned. He leant forward and rotated the spit. He didn't much care for this dog-eating business, but there it was: they had to eat something. So he tended to his duties, although he himself now had very little appetite. The alcohol had dulled the hunger in his stomach. And now his solitude and tiredness prompted him to relax and rest. He could now have been sitting comfortably in his armchair at home, re-reading perhaps his favourite classical myths. The boy would have been sound asleep while he, urged on by Aphrodite, would have touched his beloved who, drowsy and uncomplaining, bestowed upon him her divine womanly warmth…

Having felt her warmth for a too fleeting moment, he was suddenly shivering with cold. While he had been carried away by dreams, the fire had reduced itself to a smoulder. How he longed to go away! he thought, while he did nothing about the fire but continued to shiver. This place turned men into beasts. It crushed them, gnawed them up and shat them out. Not that he was going anywhere. Everyone got what was coming to him. No one could escape, and perhaps there was nowhere to escape to anyway. This was the last stop: you got off and stayed there. You worked, drank and expected death. If he hadn't needed money, he would never have set foot here.

He *would* get out – once he'd made enough money. The boy's eyes were getting worse by the day. He knew it all too well. That's why he had to stay and work until he had earned enough. Strange thing: everybody seemed to have come for the money, but no one ever left. Perhaps there was some sort of irresistible spell about the place. It carried you away like a stream and swirled you into the deep before you knew it, just as the doleful river Acheron bore away the souls of the dead. He felt he was being carried away, too. He did not know what it was that bore him, but could sense some indefinable, indifferent volume of darkness. Perhaps already it was too late to go back? There was some significance in the way that death had missed him twice, flashing him a petrifying smile. A destiny to be here, to… ah! The brandy must have softened his brain. Of course there was time to go back. He just had to work his balls off until he saved the damn money. Then he would go and force it down the throat of the fucking doctor he'd pleaded with, as long as it wasn't too late.

Of course, money could be borrowed. If he told the other fellows all about it, they were bound to offer to lend him some. (Why hadn't he done it before?) True, he didn't feel completely comfortable with the idea, but what was there to be ashamed of? Tomorrow, as soon as everyone had sobered up, he would try to broach the matter.

Otherwise the child was well, he knew from the letter. That was something positive to give him the energy he needed. Before leaving, he had felt unaccountably weak all the time, and indifferent to everything. He'd turn up at school and teach classes on autopilot, without doing any of the preparation he knew he should have. Sometimes he thought that every single student was staring at him the same way, except that one of them would be a boy with eyes that were wide open and quite dead. As he looked harder at this boy he would see it was his son. He was worried all the time, at work and at home, everywhere.

Once they took Mario to an old hag who was supposed to have healing gifts. She leant over the child, passed her hand across his forehead and started muttering incantations.

'There went seven angels whetting seven knives, carrying seven candles. The archangels Michael and

Gabriel met them and asked them: "Where goest thou, o seven angels?" And they replied: "We go to cut down the evil spirit with these knives and burn him with these candles and so remove the blood from the eyes of God's good servant Mario, today and forever.'"

Then she made the sign of the cross and declared: 'Some things are bad and others are worse.' But even seven angels didn't seem to produce any noticeable difference.

It was quiet. All Vasil could hear were the voices in the hut and the dying embers. There were no gentle choruses of crickets singing in the cool September night, as there would have been in the mountains back home, unflagging and endless like life itself. Nor were there the tired mating croaks of the frogs... He had found them in the lavatory. Dozens of them, their hind legs severed, mere half-frogs struggling hopelessly to escape from their short destiny. They crawled in all directions, feebly dragging dismembered bodies, which oozed slime and blood the while. He'd bent down and swept them into the dustpan, then dumped them down the toilet bowl. That was when he'd been an army private and found himself on frog clean-up detail while the gourmet officers feasted. Years had passed since, but he was still doing it. The dirty work, that is.

He stood up to get some logs for the dying fire. When he came back he tried the dog's leg with a small pocketknife. It needed more time. And he was aware of the numbness in his own body, he must have been sitting alone outside for an age. It was time he too went back into the warmth of the hut where the others were.

As the door creaked open, he was met by a strong smell of burning pinewood mingled with sweat. His eyes needed some time to adjust to the semidarkness inside. What illumination there was came from the old broken lamp hanging from the ceiling. It cast its light on the table and the nude, flabby female body that reclined there. Shadows divided the twin flattened hemispheres of her heavy buttocks and lewdly slid into the dark, triangular form, which gaped, between her stout, bruised thighs. A narrow waist linked her prominent hips to a narrow, bony rib cage. The left arm resting under her shoved a scrawny shoulder blade above her pockmarked back, giving her a crippled look. Pressed by the weight above, the tender white meat of her breast spilled out from beneath a hairy armpit. She was looking at the floor and chewing sunflower seeds. Greasy locks of hair hid her face so little more than colourless lips could be seen, and gappy yellow teeth between which husks were regularly spat out. Little brown cockroaches scurried along the gouged tabletop, mostly concerned with the coarse breadcrumbs that lay scattered there, but also exploring certain concavities of the reclining female body. Elsewhere, her thighs conveniently clasped half-empty bottles of brandy, inserted like candles before an altar. The four men, sitting on both sides of the table, would occasionally grab one, have a swig and then tuck it firmly back in place. They were holding playing cards, and not talking much. Their eyes slid up from their cards and across the faces of the other players, and then back. Yaskata rubbed his thin beard and dragged on a vestigial cigarette.

'Pass,' he muttered, stubbing it out on the table leg.

'Okay, pass,' chimed Gocheto, who was back in his ear-cap and a green vest, a towel tied around the waist.

They stared at Hesho. The tattered woollen blanket he was wrapped in left bare the shoulder of his arm holding the cards, displaying a tattoo of a mermaid with luxuriant hair and implausible breasts. His customary knitted cap had disappeared and bareheaded he resembled a monk from a Buddhist temple (apart from the tattoo). He glanced at them under hairless eyebrows and nodded in agreement.

'No trumps,' Sava announced.

With his jacket off, sitting in a vest gnawed by mice here and there, he was displaying his impressive arm muscles. He raised the cards to his face and thoughtfully rubbed them against his black moustache, which somehow made his biceps flex conspicuously, with lots of interesting veins. The other three exchanged curious looks but did not say anything. Sava pulled a card out and placed it on the white buttocks that were lined with stretch marks. The others, in turn, put down whatever cards they thought best. Then Sava slapped down another card with great decisiveness. This time, it seemed to take them all a lot longer to decide how to respond. He patiently waited for his turn, and then showed all his cards.

'Six spades,' he said.

Gocheto carefully spread them out along the clammy flesh, glared at them, then finally forced to acknowledge the fact, swore foully.

'Deal out, Gocheto,' Yaskata prompted.

On the dirty floor below lay Meto, flushed and sweaty. He lay bound hand and foot, rags stuffed in his mouth. His glassy eyes were fixed on the wall above him where, hanging on two rusty nails, was the now finished tapestry, the guardian angel watching over the children on the brink of the precipice. Just beneath them, part of a mise-en-scène, the little girl dozed in her child's sleep, like a scrawny curled-up kitten. Her sleep must have been troubled, for she tossed around continually. Under the lids, her eyes were rolling around in their sunken orbits, chased by some unknown internal force.

All of a sudden she opened her eyes, looked at Vasil point-blank, then just as suddenly closed them again. And at the same time, something gripped his throat. He did not know what it was, but he had a feeling of certainty that it had come from the girl's dream. It wound round his neck, threatening to strangle him. He felt its slimy cold surface envelope him, move toward his heart and then begin to claw at it. It did this with increasing violence until at last, with a searing pain, he experienced his heart being ripped out of his body. After that, he felt relief and just emptiness in his chest. His heart was no longer there. So it couldn't be beating. It was lost. The feeling of emptiness, hollowness, lingered on. It wasn't so uncomfortable, really. The only thing was that his body was growing cold. Funny, he had come in to warm up – and it was warm after all, there was the fire in the hearth, logs flaming and smouldering, the spread-eagled nude woman on the table, everything as it ought to be. She seemed happy enough munching sunflower seeds, brandy bottle up the bum, and didn't seem to feel the chill. Yet it was icy coldness that crept up his neck and penetrated his skin.

'Feeling cold?' someone asked.

'I am a bit,' he replied and slithered down, resting against the rough wall. But he was lying, just as he'd lied to the doctors who had examined him before his departure. They'd asked if he had any disorders, he'd said no, but it wasn't true. He'd had a cardiac disorder ever since he was a child, and only last year a physician had given him an electrocardiogram and told him he was seriously ill and could have angina pectoris. But he hadn't told the doctors any of that. He knew they were only asking for the record and wouldn't check properly. If he'd told them the truth, they wouldn't have let him go. But he had to get the job at any price, healthy or not. The lie had deceived the doctors, but not the disorder, which was cannier. He had another attack, excruciating and stronger than before. Myriads of fire ants seemed to be crawling over his body, biting, stinging. But curiously he didn't feel the pain – he just knew they were all over him. He tried to catch his breath but couldn't, his throat was constricted.

But actually he didn't need to breathe, it was enough to stay silent and just contemplate the sleeping girl. He studied her face properly for the first time – the features of a pure and gentle child smiling in her sleep (if a bit dishevelled). He knew that the dragon that had seized his throat had escaped from her eyes; he had seen its outline in those open but unseeing eyes. Would Mario look at him some day like that too, blind and unfathoming? No. He *would not* let it happen.

First though, he had to get rid of the dragon. Even though he wasn't breathing and there was a hollow thump in his chest. He must relax and save his strength. Then perhaps the horrible reptile would doze off and he could grip its throat and throw it away somewhere near the others. Yes, it was dozing off all right, his fingers were becoming wetter. It must be specially marked somehow, he thought, perhaps with scales of different colours, forming a pattern with a secret meaning, one that perhaps no man was able to interpret... But he could no more see it than he could grasp it. He could just sense that it was huge and heavy and knew that it ripped his flesh. If only he could at least release an arm and wipe the froth from his mouth... but then why did he have to? It could dry harmlessly on his chin. No, it was best to consider every movement carefully before taking action. There must be no mistakes. Otherwise a bad dream of a child's blindness would become the reality, and that would be unbearable.

He saw Gocheto grab an ink marker, lick it and firmly mark the score on the mother's pasty backside as the girl slept on, innocent face turned to the wall. Whether because of the saliva or the sweat, the score became smudged into a bluish green stain. Something about this smearing and the woman sprawled on the table reminded Vasil of a picture an old friend had of a butterfly perched on a flower and stuck with pins. 'Stuffed On One's Own Habitat', that's what it had been titled. Or something like that.

The cards kept being dealt out and the brandy in the bottles was being drained at a rate to match. It was becoming ever more meaningless and more heated. Vasil had never played cards and had never quite understood why some people found it such an absorbing occupation. A deficiency of some kind that required to be made up. But he ought to give it a try, too – God knew there was deficiency enough in him. Yes, he'd definitely give it a go while he had the chance. Against his nature, he also found himself fancying a cigarette. He seldom smoked, but sometimes, like now, the desire to poison his lungs was immensely appealing. If he just slipped a hand into the bulging pocket of his jacket he could pull out the packet that had been there untouched since... but he wouldn't be able to draw on any cigarette, he realized. Or reach for one. His throat had tightened again, and no nicotine would reach his lungs, smoke might hang in the air and spill through the room but nothing would fill the void he felt in his chest, where his heart was supposed to be. He seemed to be in limbo, cuddled in the womb of his mother though at the same time knowing perfectly distinctly that he was sitting with his back against this wall, and the wind, blowing through the crack of the door, was tickling his earlobe, just *there*. He had a similar feeling when he made love to his wife, a sort of exalted intensity. He sank down between her comfortable pink thighs and at the same time soared up. But she wasn't there now. If she had been, she would have taken care of him, tried to save him even if deep down she knew it was hopeless.

None of the foursome around the table paid any attention to him, as if he had vanished into space. In a way, he preferred it like that. He could sit and keep watching, without imposing himself on anyone. To be quiet and still was probably the best course for him in the circumstances. Otherwise the dragon might become annoyed and decide to finish him off there and then. Hidden in the dusk, he would wait. Perhaps the morning sun would chase it away. September nights here were long, but the important thing was to be patient so as eventually to break free.

Something on the ground flashed. Meto, still lying next to the hearth, was looking at him glassily, his eyes like tiny splinters pointing at him. He realized he had seen him, and had been watching him all the time. So there was someone who would be able to point at him and say: 'Look everyone, Vasil isn't breathing!' But at the moment Meto wasn't likely to do that. Smoke was coming from the rags stuffed in his mouth. The left part of his face had gone scarlet and was in fact burning.

The smoke rose in clouds and with it the smell of scorched hair. It crawled over the gamblers, dropped down and obliterated their cards with faintly yellowish wafts. They sniffed, looked at each other and sniffed again.

'Something burning,' Gocheto said. They got to their feet, sniffing some more at the smoke. It irritated their nostrils and made their eyes smart. Down on the floor, from where the smoke was coming, they noticed him. Grunting, nostrils aflame, eyes rolled back. They bent down and touched the body.

'He's burnt,' someone observed.

They poured water on him. It was absorbed by the parched skin and vanished into the pores. The smoke disappeared along with the water. Lida had sat up, slightly twisted on the table as for a life class, her dry flabby breasts with their pale nipples hanging pitifully. The men lifted poor Meto and placed him on a hewn log, used as a stool. Once unsupported, he lurched and then slid smoothly down between Lida's open legs. They hoicked him back up, pulled the charred rags from his mouth and filled it with brandy, which vanished quickly down his throat. His pupils rolled back where they should be, seemed to expand momentarily and then to shrink. He gritted his yellow ill-spaced teeth and snorted loudly and messily. Then he took a deep breath and people waited to see what would happen next. Then he said something.

'Scared you, huh?' They stood there, staring at him in silence. Poor Meto grinned and went on, his charred voice rasping nastily.

'I'll set you on fire! I'll burn you all!' A mocking dimple twitched on his parched cheek. Sava leaned forward and stuffed the rags back into his mouth and the dimple disappeared.

'He's bonkers,' Hesho explained to no one in particular and, shoving Lida back down on the table, resumed dealing the cards.

So Meto remained in that position, propped up between the stout legs of the whore reclining in front of him. Vasil could see the man's knobbly spine, the coarse sinewy arms bound with rope, and their shadow, which fell on the floor and almost touched his own. He could easily stretch out a hand and loosen the loop that bit into the shadow wrists. No one would know. No one cared about shadows. They were fleshless, fastened to the ground crawling around with you until in an instant they would bid you adieu. They went on, unencumbered, towards the kingdom of Hades and left you lying stiff in some dark corner. His shadow decided to slither across while it had the chance to untie the loop of the other's; delicately, as shadows can. Yes, there it was, it had set him free. So why didn't he take flight? What was he waiting for? Get away, why don't you, before the others realize what's happened! But he didn't. He remained as he was without a single stir, just an odd groan that pushed thickly through the charred rags.

Meanwhile, the dragon had shifted its grip on Vasil's throat. He seemed to feel, or hear, one of the vertebrae in his neck crack. His shadow stirred, sniffing a prospect of escape, but remained where it was for the time being. Time for another few hands of cards, at least. A deficiency of some kind that required to be made up. He might get away with it yet, you never could tell.

Gocheto took the ink marker from behind his ear and scrawled something on the shifting buttocks that formed the focus of the gamblers' attention. The bluish green stain had smudged and oozed down the woman's flanks in gangrenous trickles. Slithering across her body, the sweaty liquor paused on the tabletop before dribbling down and spilling onto the men's legs and their shadows on the floor.

Vasil suddenly knew what it was. The green everything had seemed to be in the army. Everything – people, houses, flowers, birds, guns, sky, stars, sounds (could that be right? it seemed so at the time). The grass of course was especially green, just as grass ought to be. Even in autumn. But autumn grass is not green. The army had required it to be, though, so he and the others had been ordered to spray the entire barracks with green paint. They sprayed and sprayed, all day and all night. Next morning, every surface was covered with a greasy layer of green gunk. In his nightmares since then, he would find himself fleeing from an enormous avalanche of green paint that swept blindly towards him, trying to drown him and clog his pores and eyes and claim him for greenness. The whore on the table had been claimed already, green flowing from her matted hair in green waves over her green body, while the men around the green table scowled at their green cards. (Not a very nice green either, dull and dirty.)

Oblivious to all this the girl slept on, alone in her dreams and disregarded by all except Vasil. She had fallen asleep with legs uncovered. If he had been able to, he would have tucked them in for her, as he always used to do for Mario in the winter nights before he went to bed himself. Then he would lean forward and kiss his son, and Mario would respond with a frown before returning to his dream. Children needed a great deal of care. Otherwise they went wild, became beasts that would one day be locked up in a cage, like the one that now trapped him, and from which he must escape and go back home. His wife must be having a hard time coping on her own. A mother is no substitute for a father, especially where a son is concerned. Sons should be close to their fathers until they become men themselves. It reassures them and gives them strength – the sons of course, but the fathers too. A good thing that his son couldn't see his father as he was now, though. But then he would already be asleep, just like this wretched child with her tiny bare feet. If he could only move, he would have tried to tuck her in. The logs in the hearth were burning out and no one had thought of throwing more on to make the fire revive. But it was still warm enough in the hut, for now.

The men went on drinking and playing cards. They had another crate of brandy in reserve. He knew that they would stay up like that, working their way through the cards and the booze, until dawn. The constant dealing and re-dealing of cards got on his nerves, but he followed it mechanically, not really knowing why. The cards were shuffled, separated, reunited, disorganized and organized. Little but the sounds of the cards broke the silence.

'I'm hungry,' someone said in the gap between two games. Hesho got up, took the knife, passed him by and went out. The cold rushed inside, had a quick look round and then went outside again. Was it looking for someone in particular? Surely it must have come for him. It might have intended to suck out what little warmth was left in his body. It had gone for now, but only to return another time and finish him off then. The doctors had long been preparing him for the eventuality. One day he would be left without a heart, and he would just have to make the best of it. But this would be the worst possible time to fall prey to the deathly cold – when he had to get to his feet, roll up his sleeves, make five thousand roubles and get back home quick. Of course, he knew he was kidding himself. There was never a right time. Or rather, there was never a wrong time. It was all the same, one moment as good or bad as any other. Let bygones be bygones. That's all that can be expected of you, and then one day you feel the cold crawl up your body and it's enough.

Hesho came back, and though the door was closed quite slowly, Death didn't take the opportunity to follow him in. Only the night peeped in for a moment. Hesho's bare tattooed arm held the knife upright like a candle, with rare (not to say bleeding) morsels skewered on it. He had obviously lopped them off from the hind legs, careful to secure the choicest cuts. They quivered on the blade, until he turned it downward and drove it into the corner of the table. Then he carefully slipped them off and wrenched the knife out. He took a piece of meat for himself and deposited the other hot, greasy chunks on Lida's behind, which she wasn't expecting.

'Help yourselves!' he invited them, pulling at the tough meat with his big teeth. The fat smeared his hairless chin, which glowed in the light of the flame. He smacked his lips and clicked his tongue, and little doggy sinews briefly protruded from his mouth before disappearing again. This happened several times. He chomped away at the meat very thoroughly, no doubt eager to extract all the deliciousness he could, then unceremoniously spat most of it out. A much-masticated lump flew past the face of Meto, still sitting on his log, and fell in his shadow.

Vasil felt the same urge: to spit on his own shadow, against the evil eye, in the hope that grim Charon would pass by. But he couldn't do it; he couldn't even manage to dribble. His saliva settled, gathered and filled the cavity of his mouth – somewhat thick and dried, like clotted blood. Yes, it could be blood. Something was flowing down his sinuses, salty and best got rid of. But it tasted of life. If he let it go, he saw it returning to

snake round his neck, a dragon-blasted noose of snot
and spit and blood to throttle him.

He was watching this group of men, gathered in a
circle around the table, munching away at their dog.
They grunted as they munched. Actually not pigs but
people. Ordinary people, workers, having a party as best
they could. Brought together by blind fate, they were
celebrating. But they were doing this slowly and silently
and not that happily, waiting for time to pass and take
them along with it, somewhere else.

Gocheto had started telling a story.

'One day a camel turned up in the village,' he said,
'No one knew how or where it came from. It just stood
there in the village square chewing the cud. The whole
village came out to see it. They wondered what that
thing with the two humps could be, but didn't have a
clue. Someone said it must be Stoyo's mare that had
disappeared in the woods the previous year. Someone
else chimed in that no it wasn't Stoyo's mare that had
disappeared in the woods – it had hatched from an egg
he'd found in the coop. This egg had been ten times
the size of the other eggs. He'd taken the egg and given
it to his wife to hatch. She'd put it in her lap and kept
it warm there nine days until she could restrain herself
no longer and had to go to the loo. She placed the egg
on a couch and covered it with a rug. When she came
back and lifted the rug, the egg had gone. So that's the
creature that hatched from the egg, he said. No – a
third chap said – that's not Stoyo's mare that

disappeared in the woods last year, nor did it hatch from an egg ten times the size of other eggs, it was that cloud he'd seen over the village last summer which looked just like it. He'd gazed and gazed at that cloud, and he'd seen it reach the mountaintop, then climb down and start roaming around all over the place. The villagers argued on and on, until they decided to ask the oldest and wisest of them all (who was a hundred years old and had been to town three times). They called on the old man and told him what they had seen in the square. He lowered his head, stroked his beard and was lost in thought for a long time. At last he declared with all his authority that it was most certainly a hundred-year-old hare.'

Finishing his story, Gocheto took the only remaining full bottle between the female thighs, raised it and poured the contents down his throat. He gave a loud snort, pulled his ear-flapped cap as far back as it could go, took a deep breath, leaned forward and sank his teeth into the tabletop. The sinews on his neck stood out, his veins swelled with blood and he lifted up the table with the woman still on it. The bottles wobbled and then fell on the floor, shattering into a myriad tiny splinters. Lida didn't scream. She just lay there with the look of a frightened beast, holding on by her nails that were dug into the wood. Gocheto, his eyes screwed up, growled furiously and shook the table. She lost her grip, slid down on her back and was deposited at the feet of the others, panting, breasts heaving, her spread-eagled figure with a rufous triangle bristling between her white legs. Gocheto stood there, his teeth still firmly sunk into the table. All of a sudden, a deep growl welled up from his chest. As the growl gradually developed a kind of rhythm, he started dancing – an ancient chain dance. He threw his chest out, the vest sweatily glued to it, his arms trailing behind. His tread was deliberate and heavy. The splinters of glass scattered on the floor cut into his bare feet and left a trail of blood, and with each successive beat it widened further, until a bloodily smeared ring was described.

Vasil was listening to the crackle of the glass. Gocheto's feet were big and dirty white, with yellow nails, jagged like the glass. They stepped forward and spattered blood towards him, moving slowly and stickily, as if in limbo. All this was like a strange dream from which he wanted to escape, to wake up in bed to the smell of freshly washed bed linen, an ironed pillow under his head and his wife's warm body at his side. But it wasn't a dream. The only dream was that of the girl, the one the dragon had escaped from to steal his heart. The girl herself slept on, deeply and peacefully, under the outspread wings of the guardian angel in the tapestry hanging on the wall. Perhaps if she woke up, the monster that held fast his heart would dissolve with her dream? But let her stay sleeping. It was all right by him. He prayed for her and he prayed that the dream would continue to keep the smile on her face.

'Stop it!' Yaskata cried out. He leapt up, his jacket sliding from his shoulders and dropping on the ground like a scarecrow. He sprang forward and grabbed the table. Gocheto flexed his shoulders with a menacing growl and didn't let go. His body shook, and then the table moved unsteadily backwards.

'That's enough,' said Yaskata, in a clear, steady voice. But his eyes were narrowed in a squint, and his facial muscles were twitching.

Abruptly, he yanked the table out from Gocheto's mouth, together with several teeth. The growl was cut short. Gocheto stopped dead in his tracks. Blood trickled from the side of his mouth, crawled down his chin and dribbled on the floor, where it mixed with the blood from his cut feet. He looked up and smiled, but it was a sardonic smile, forced and bloody.

'Cuckold!' he spat out.

They were standing on either side of the table, breathing hard and glaring at each other. Gocheto decisively hurled the table away, but they stayed facing each other as if it was still there.

'Cuckold!' he repeated and was answered by hard punch in the belly. He roared, doubled up and then lurched forward, burrowing his head into his adversary's chest. Yaskata was forced to take a step backward before grabbing Gocheto by the scruff of the neck and bashing his face into his knee. Stunned and unbalanced, Gocheto collapsed on the ground. Shards of glass were pushed through his vest and lacerated his back. Yaskata stood over him, waiting, but the fallen man did not get up.

'Cuckold!' Gocheto mouthed. 'Your wife's a whore! Trash like you!'

'Say that again!'

'She's a whore! And the cheapest, too!'

Yaskata silenced him with a hard kick between the legs.

Vasil had watched them fighting. Gocheto had fallen just inches from his feet. He heard the thump as his head struck the floor. It was the same thump a log made when it fell from a height. But he couldn't help him. His legs disobeyed him and so he remained where he was. The others just sat there too, and he imagined they might be crying. Large yellowish tears that flowed down their cheeks and poured onto the floor, washing away the blood.

This was a vision. In reality, there were no tears. There was nothing but fear in the air and silence. Except that someone was whispering, in the corner of the room. It was like the whisper of lizards. As a child he had seen them in the summer, popping out from their holes and lying on the warm stones, opening their mouths at the sun and reflexing their bluish throats and whispering. But there was nothing in the corner. And outside was only the night, clear and freezing cold.

Then he realized that what he had heard was the moans of the dragon. Poor reptile, they must have hit it, or squashed it with the table. Well, it would just have to bear it. After all, he himself had to bear it, didn't he? It could leave him alone and go wherever it was dragons went. Perhaps it had no home? Were there old homeless dragons? Anyway, better if it went and became someone else's problem.

The girl cried out. When he looked at the bed, she lay calmly enough, eyes closed and still asleep. But nevertheless she had cried out – screamed, even. He had heard it clearly. A child's scream, sharp and ringing. Children were apt to scream in their sleep; Mario did. Sometimes he even wept... What did they dream of? Things they had never seen – witches, balls of fire, dragons and other monsters. They appeared out of the blue and chased them, then vanished into the abyss whence they came. He remembered it well. That's how it had been in his childhood, and that's how it was for everyone. When you are young, you dream. Later you have no time for it and everything goes according to the routine, until the routine also ends and you fall in an eternal sleep, with no dreams. It was so long since he had had a dream. He just fell asleep at night and woke up the next morning. As if the night had lasted no more than a second; no time for a dream, a nightmare or a caress. But he would finally get it – the Dark. Abundantly, and forever. Some people were even treated to it during their lifetime. His son, for example.

The girl slept on. It was good that she was asleep. But why had she cried out? A nightmare, yes, of course. But if she woke up now, my God, what would she see?

The very thought of it! Let her sleep and not see it. *But she's seen it all before.* How could he say that to himself? How could that thought which he was afraid to think still have crossed his mind? But then, fear isn't voluntary. Anything but her seeing, he thought. Sleep, sleep, my little girl...

Her mother lay spreadeagled on the far side of the floor, at the feet of the men. She smelt the fear in the air and her breath quickened. She got up from her uncomfortable position and crouched on all fours, her back arched like a cat. She started trembling, and her face became contorted, but still she remained apprehensively at their feet.

Meto turned his half-burnt body and gawked at her. Though repulsive, there was also something seductive even in that aging, flabby body. It was still a woman, a human of the opposite sex, with all a woman's distinctive physical features and smells and undeniable attractions. He imagined he was smiling at her. And it wasn't a leer. But then it wasn't any sort of smile: just a mouth stuffed with charred rags. Nevertheless, something flitted across his face and stopped at the corners of his eyes. Bound to the chair, in his thoughts Meto slowly ran his hand all along her back. But she was oblivious to his caress and remained as she was, on all fours, bristling and arched like a cat in heat.

Sava grabbed her by the hair and yanked her aside. He seemed to exude strength and self-confidence. He took one step forward, paused, and then took another.

'That's enough, Yaskata,' he warned. Yaskata, who still had hold of the barely conscious Gocheto, turned round like a predator over its prey, angry to be disturbed. He was crouched, ready to leap.

'None of your business,' he answered brusquely.

'Why did you do it?'

'He was picking a fight!'

'You're lying.'

Yes, he was lying all right, Vasil decided. Of course, you can never be completely sure about these things. You can only have a feeling about them. Various rumours, intertwining with each other, directed you to one and the same thing. The truth. It spawned them and destroyed them, with its singular authenticity and, in a way, meaninglessness. Often things are simple in themselves, but the relationships between them make for hopeless confusion.

There she was, between them. He had never seen her before, but he knew it must be her. She didn't look at anybody, just smiled shyly. Her face seemed waxen and pockmarked. She was crouching, with her head lowered and hair loose. It was an indefinite metal colour and had a peculiar gloss. Her dress clung to her body, clarifying her figure. She lifted her hands from her knees and pushed her hair back behind the ears. The face now better revealed was unusually clean and unlined, and her complexion smoother than it had looked before. It was difficult to tell her age. Some women didn't have an age, they stayed the same, especially if they smiled like that.

He knew this was Yaskata's wife, the same woman he had once brought here, and the one that was now walking out on him. The others had never spoken about any of it when he was there. Not till then anyway.

'He's right,' Sava told him.

'Go on.'

They were stalking each other: first words, then actions.

She had been long gone, yet she remained between them, there in time and space, smiling. Really she was very ordinary looking, the sort of woman you wouldn't look at twice. But there was something about her, hard to say what exactly, that attracted you. They said she was a flirt, but no one had actually seen her behaving that way. Whatever the truth was, it wasn't any of his business, Vasil had decided. But there is always another side to things, a counterpart. Acting as irritants to each other, they ensure things build up, like calluses.

He had never much concerned himself with the petty arguments between the other men. Although over time he noticed his thoughts increasingly turning toward them. Working together – and tough work at that – meant you had to co-operate. But the same things that brought you together would sometimes produce friction. They would become more outspoken, sometimes shouting at each other, and once in a while that would turn into a fight. Usually everything would be back to normal shortly afterwards – save a lingering fear that the foreman might hear about it and fire them for misconduct. However, there were recognized danger areas and they did their best to avoid those. In any case, Vasil had enough worries of his own and had no wish to get involved – not that he could very well have done so anyway. He was a mere onlooker, a man whose business was his sure progress to the other world.

And although he could see well enough (surprising for a man almost dead), he could hardly hear anything; there was a funny noise in his ears much of the time and the only completely clear sound was the crackle of the fire. Now and then the noise vanished and he could hear and understand clearly, whether he wished to or, more likely, didn't. The pain in his chest, as he sat on the floor, overwhelmed him and made him an involuntary witness to what was going on. The sick are indifferent to other people. Pain makes you bitter and selfish. You don't give a damn what the living may get up to, you're not one of them any longer. They can look after themselves. What could you do anyway, cold, convulsed and clapped out, peering out of your poky corner? All you can do – all you are required to do – is to attend to your own cross.

He knew he ought to slow down. That chilly slime around his chest could slither out of the skin; gather up its guts and go. Then his heart would go back into its proper place and start beating all over again. He thought he sensed the dragon to be losing some vigour, though the noose was still twisted tight. And if it were twisted yet tighter, so be it. What was the damn thing waiting for? Why so slow? It had left the job half-done.

Bad luck, that's what he'd always had. Now this monster from the dream had dumped him. Leaving him neither dead nor alive. Life didn't hold out great attractions. Really it would be better if was all over and done with as soon as possible, so he could have lost his heavy burden, lost himself in the realm of shadows, rested and found peace that would never be disturbed...

But there was the boy. He couldn't leave him like that. Those damned eyes, why were they failing? It should have been him instead. There was nothing he much needed to see any more. Only thirty-four, but life seemed to have been over long ago. He'd got married, then Mario had been born, and ever since then it had just been things repeating themselves. People, work, cares, problems, domestic spats, even the position in which – albeit seldom – they made love at night. It was all painfully familiar: the people in the streets, the way to work, the furniture at home, and the woman he went to bed with. Blindness wouldn't disturb him, not at all. It made no difference whether he could see or indeed whether he was alive. But it was only just starting for the child. He had to study and make it in life, rather than remain a misfit who invited pity. The child had to make it. And, provided he got the right treatment, he would.

Which was why he'd come to work in that god-awful place. If anyone needed or wanted his heart, they'd be welcome to it. But not just yet. Right now, it would be fine if he got away and this dragon fucked off. He felt it slithering. It could have cut itself on the glass on the floor and decided to make off for repairs. Who knows? He couldn't see it. He'd probably only see it when he crossed over to the other side (if these things happened). Then the thought struck him that perhaps it had chosen someone else.

The two men remained as they had been, face to face. The weak light from the gas lamp cast a circle around them, like a boxing ring, but more claustrophobic. Had they reached out, they could have touched each other, but they didn't budge. They just stood glaring at each other, their eyebrows lowered in frowns, without speaking, looking for something in each other's eyes – truth perhaps, or a weak point.

'Have you ever been with her?' Yaskata demanded in a whisper.

'Many times,' Sava replied. He said it in a firm, even voice, without embarrassment.

'You admit it!'

'You never asked before.'

'I hate you!' he bellowed.

It was a load roar, almost inhuman. He lunged forward and hit Sava hard in the temple with his right fist. Then he kneed him between the legs, and his left fist struck him in the side, low under the kidneys. When he hit again with his right it was a powerful uppercut to the chin. Sava went back, doubled up, and covered his face with his fists until he had recovered from the pain of the blows, then leapt up and with his long muscular reach shoved Yaskata in the chest. Stepping back, he tried to keep his balance, but

Gocheto's sprawling body tripped him and he collapsed on top of him. When he tried to get up, Sava's left fist hit him back. Sava bent down over him, grabbed him under the armpits and rammed him against the wall.

They stood above Vasil's head, to his right. Snarling like boars, stinking of brandy, sweat and bad teeth. Out of the corner of his eye he saw Sava hoick the other man up, scraping his back against the wall. He held him tightly under the armpits, arms helplessly flailing around and head twisted. Sava's muscles bulged and sweat streamed down his sinewy neck and, absorbed by his vest, formed a dark trail along his spine. But he did not let him go. Standing so, legs braced, leaning into the wall, he reminded Vasil of Hercules crushing Antaeus, holding him above the Earth, which was his strength. The fire was dying out. The embers crept along the hearth, twinkling. 'Throw us something!' they seemed to beg. 'Throw us something – or someone – and we'll turn them into fire!'

He rolled his eyes back towards the men. Yaskata was hanging, limp and almost lifeless, his eyes closed and head rolling. But his heart was beating strongly, in heavy thumps, sending pulses through his body as the wind might course through the branches of a tree. Sava shrugged his powerful shoulders, lowered his arms and freed his antagonist, and Yaskata slipped down and rested against the base of the wall.

Vasil peered around the room, trying to find her, but she wasn't there. She had melted into the darkness, taking her mysterious femininity and her smile with her. Only an afterglow remained, almost imperceptibly illuminating the coarse darkness of the hut. But that too was waning, and was on the point of extinction when its vestiges were blotted by the less faint scent of almonds.

They grew across the river, on the hillside. When they were children they used to go there and gather them in their pockets. When they cracked them between cobblestones in the street, they split and there were the kernels – twins, very often. They would chew them and enjoy the crunchiness and the particular flavour. Rather like the present one, which was certainly nice and crunchy, but the flavour was less ... well, less like an almond really.

The cockroaches were crawling over him. They had slipped under his clothes and were now delicately feeling him with their antennae. Were they looking for something to eat or just trying to find a place to lay their eggs? He wanted to squash them, but the only thing he could do was watch them move up and down his body. They were all over the floor, even on Gocheto's sprawled body, licking his blood as it flowed. He lay there open-mouthed, a furred tongue hanging out. His face was contorted and swollen, his back and the soles of his feet bleeding. With a writhing movement, he rolled over face down and drew his arms in, pushing them under his chest. Straining his muscles, he tried to get up, but fell back onto the glass-strewn floor. After a pause to gather strength, he tried again. Gradually his elbows straightened and he moved onto his knees that, like the palms of his hands, were pressed by his weight into the glass. Every part of him was spattered with blood.

Sava carefully lifted him up, placed him on Yaskata's vacant bed and sat down by his side.

'Brandy,' Gocheto groaned.

Sava bent down, pulled out a bottle from under the bed, unscrewed the top and brought the bottle to his lips. Gocheto gulped the liquid down, screwed his eyes up, and then went limp.

Lida pulled herself up to rest against the bed, her nudity pallid and wanton. She slid her hand up Gocheto's thighs; when she got to the groin her hand slowed momentarily, then went up the belly. It stopped on his chest, and her podgy fingers were feeling around something with unusual care. She deftly extricated a piece of glass that had stuck between his ribs and threw it behind her without looking. It fell in the folds of the blanket that Hesho was wrapped in. After a moment, some movement of his brought it into contact with his skin. He shivered, groped around inside the blanket and located the piece. Held up to the light, it was visibly sticky with blood. He examined it carefully, at the same time making strange clicking sounds with his tongue. Then he suddenly popped it in his mouth and crunched it up with his big teeth.

The crunching grated on Vasil's ears and penetrated his body instead of the Gypsy's, digging into the cavity of his chest. It had to be a deep incision, because it hurt. The pain crawled up from his midriff toward his heart. He told himself it was an illusion, that the pain was not real. Then he felt the scales of the dragon scratching his skin. Something was thumping and beating and he realized it was his heart. It was a hollow and dull beat, but it was nevertheless his beat. This is how he had known it ever since childhood, when he would place his hand on his chest to feel it beating. Many years had passed since then, and his heart had grown up with him, had become tired like him, but still it beat on and on. Once he had thought it would go on forever, without end. But no, it had turned out that there was an end. It could be brought on anywhere and by anything, even by an imaginary dragon that had escaped from a child's eyes. The eyes of a child doomed to see what God didn't much care to.

The girl was still asleep, curled up in a ball, absorbed in her dream, small and helpless in this world. How he longed to help, to do something to save her from her nightmares. But what could an ordinary dying man like himself do for anyone? A man powerless even to save his own child from banishment to the realm of the Prince of Darkness. Still, there must be something to be done for us all, even if only as slight as a man's strength and senses. He watched her crossly wrinkle her snub nose then pull her tiny hand (with polished nails) from between her legs and rub it. But whatever was annoying her apparently didn't go away; for she rolled over to the other side, then back, then again and again. At the same time, something shook him and he felt the monster shift and snake towards someone else, and he felt his soul was free again.

He heard a whimper, immediately thought it was her, then realized it was Meto. The madman was straining his limbs, blowing out his cheeks through the rags that gagged him, and whining with the effort. He was tossing around from side to side as he struggled desperately to untie himself. Vasil looked at Sava to see if he realized what was happening, but he was sitting beside the whore, facing the other way. They were bent over Gocheto and seemed deaf to all else. Then he watched as Meto, free at last, stealthily slipped out of the shadows and reached carefully for the knife that had been driven into the table. He pulled it out, crept up behind the unsuspecting Sava's back and then savagely thrust the knife in, up to the hilt, to the left and just under the shoulder blade.

The girl screamed, woke up and opened her eyes. Something thumped in Vasil's chest and he felt his heart in place, beating wildly. Searing pain. His chest seemed to be filling up and he gasped for breath. He tried to struggle to his feet but found himself giddily slumping back with his ears ringing. Then everything became quiet. He saw Sava turn round and raise himself up to his full height, his elbows bent behind his back and his head up stretched. He tried to get hold of the knife, but his hands blindly scrabbled in vain and the blade remained buried in him. Blood was spurting out from the wound, drenching the blue and white stripes of his vest. He tugged at his big black moustache, and then doubled up.

'Even if you see it, don't believe it!' he warned, his dark eyes now laden with unshed tears. Then he crumpled and crashed onto the floor.

Vasil strained and scrambled to his feet, dashed forward and knelt by Sava. Blood was continuing to flow from the wound, but he could detect no heartbeat. Sava stared at him with open and lifeless eyes. Vasil raised his hand, now stained with blood, and closed them. He remained on his knees, face to face with the dead man. The cold sweat on his neck, the scales of the dragon, the shadowy flight of a departing spirit. It was all-familiar. There was a sudden breeze, and he thought he could again smell almonds. His eyes sought out the girl. She stood there, snuggling against her mother's naked body. She was peering with tired eyes over Lida's shoulder, unblinking and dazed. And above them the guardian angel watched over the children of God, wings protectively outspread as ever.

He looked toward Yaskata, who stood there, slightly stooping, blood-spattered, and eyes bloodshot. Feeling the gaze on him, he started, glared around like a beast, turned, pushed open the door and disappeared outside. The cold rushed into the room and smiled with its brittle and icy smile. Vasil got up and followed him. Outside, the night sparkled, crystal-clear and implacably serene. This mortal world had been walled in by an infinity of gleaming stars which no doubt pointed the way to a truth as eternal as it was hopeless.

He looked down at his feet. Legs wide apart, he stood over the fire. It had died out. This had only incensed the dog, which hung there, spitted, its underside charred, staring with its nasty dead head.

* * *

He lowered his head toward the coffin and the dead man lying in it. On his back, arms crossed on the chest, cold and stiff, he was waiting for them to put the lid on. Peaceful, free of worry, with eyes closed and mouth half-open, he looked like a man with time to spare. No problems and no blood. His blood had all disappeared down the greedy gullet of Thanatos. His skin, having lost its hue, had become the colour of asphodel. His features were clean and clear, purified by the beauty of death. Men stabbed in the back are handsome. They die properly. They get on with it. They don't cry for help or burst into tears, but clench their teeth and bite their black moustaches. Death loves men and men love death, or ought to. It makes them manlier than living men, their faces whiter, their hair blacker, and their bodies heavier. Just a pity that they're dead, really.

They had to close the coffin. Time was running out. It would be dark any moment, and the train was leaving tomorrow. Looking at him was useless. The thing to do was close the coffin and seal it. Lead coffins are always sealed, loaded on the train and forgotten. But someone had to take care of the body. Those at the hospital didn't have much time for the dead. They certified whether it was murder or an accident, and then handed them over to the others – fellow workers, friends, or (unlikely, this) family – to do what they could. Some wretches departed just as they were, having no one to wash away the blood and clean them up. They were pushed in the coffin, face up or face down, and despatched home. Who would see them inside? Who would know if it was a son, a husband or indeed a human being at all? And afterwards at the funeral, the family might well weep and wonder at whose grave they were mourning. That's how things were. And that's what the law said: 'Lead coffins are not to be opened.' You get the coffin with the name inscribed on the lid. 'Accident,' they'll tell you, but there he lies, stabbed in the back.

Blood was hard to get rid of. It had taken time for the body to be examined by the police, the doctors, and then the foreman, and in the meanwhile the blood hardened. Having neither surgical spirit nor after-shave, they scrubbed him clean with a towel soaked in brandy. So now the whole morgue stank of it, and it originated, with other smells, from the dead man's body. The room was small and cold, and the cold was good, because it blunted the stench somewhat. It was the first time Vasil had been inside the morgue, though most of the workers went to the hospital regularly to be tested for syphilis. It was a bit to the side of the main building, a wooden annex with no heating, so the cold found a place by the bodies. It must have been the only accident lately, since poor Sava had the place to himself. So if it hadn't happened, the morgue would have been empty now. And Sava might easily not have died, they could have avoided the fight, they could have avoided getting drunk in the first place. Sava could have been somewhere else entirely – in the south, where life was lived in full measure and there was no lechery or drunkards, no hatred or killing, and flowers and kindness instead of foul, stagnant swamps. Yes, he could easily have stayed alive. He could have dodged death. He could have had a family and a house full of children.

As it was he'd had no close relations, it seemed, except the knife in his back. They were asked if he had any family to take delivery of the body. But no one knew anything; he got no letters and had never mentioned anyone. Funny thing, but it was only now that they thought about it. He'd always seemed so calm and strong and straightforward. Even when he was in a bad mood and fierce with the others, they still respected him.

Vasil remembered how as soon as he had joined the work team, Sava had thrown him a spade and urged, 'Down to work!' So without being asked twice he'd waded right into the concrete. When he tried to break free, it was heavier than he'd thought, and he felt something crack in the small of his back; a pain shot up the spine and right to the back of his neck. He'd limped over to the side, some distance from the casing, and leant on his spade. The foreman had seen him, walked up angrily and yelled at him: 'You there, the newcomer – stop lazing around or go home!'

'It hurts,' he had replied.

'This ain't no hospital,' the foreman had cackled. But his spine hurt like hell. What could he do? At home they were expecting him back soon. The child couldn't wait. He was going blinder every day. Mario was not to blame for being ill, and shouldn't suffer because his father had a weak back. Then he had heard a steady, deep voice affirm, 'You're staying,' Sava had said it loudly so everyone would hear. The foreman gave him a resentful look. 'Your business,' he grunted. 'You do his work if you're that stupid.' So he'd stayed in the team, eventually recovered, got used to the physical labour and pretty soon was working as hard as the rest of them. He should have thanked Sava. He had wanted to but he never did, for fear of looking ridiculous. Now it didn't seem ridiculous at all but it was too late. He missed Sava. They all did. No one had said it, but they all recognized that they'd felt safe with him there. You needed someone to lean on, so you could take a deep breath and keep going. But Sava was dead. A stupid mistake, and he wouldn't be doing anything for anyone now. They'd try their best to manage without him, but you could see it wasn't going to work out well.

Several hours after the stabbing, the foreman had strode into the hut and glared at the body. 'What a pain in the neck,' he remarked. He stared at them all with a contemptuous smile but didn't add to his comment. Then he pulled from his inside pocket a crumpled wad of papers folded in two, leafed through them, clicked his pen noisily and announced: 'I'm going to cross him out from the list.' And he did.

They were asked to pack his things; they were only expected to give the management the address of friends or relatives if they found one. The coffin ought to be delivered to someone who knew him. Otherwise it would have to go to the local authority, which would foot the bill. They tried to remember if he had ever mentioned any relatives or loved ones. They racked their brains, but in vain. It was a blank. Could he really have been all alone, having no one who'd be expecting him back? That's how it looked. In his things they found nothing, not a single letter, not even a single line addressed to him. Except that right at the bottom of his bag laid one old, yellowing snapshot.

Vasil held the photograph up to see it better, and realized who it was. It was her, the woman who had haunted the room, redolent of almonds. She was sitting on Sava's knee, held fast in his big arms, and they were laughing and gazing into each other's eyes. She looked just as he had seen her the time before, but it was a much younger Sava, his skin smooth and clean-shaven, his hair cropped short with a fringe. He was in a light, loose shirt and baggy black trousers. Vasil looked at the girl again, but this time he began to have doubts; he thought he might be mistaken, that he was looking at some woman who just happened to bear a strong – a very strong – resemblance to the other one. So he handed the snapshot across for everyone else to see. They took it, looked at each other in bewilderment and whispered: 'It can't be'. But ... it was her, Yaskata's wife. Strange how big and how small the world could be, for everyone to know a woman who belonged to no one.

Sava was lying in the midst of them in his metal coffin, unshrouded but wrapped instead in a black blanket that brought to Vasil's mind the poisoned covering of the centaur Nessus. It had been hard enough getting even that old tat from the commissary. 'We're short of blankets for the living and you want one for the dead,' the old trout had grumbled, but ultimately let him have one for which even she could conceive no other use. They'd wrapped him carefully, right up to the armpits, to hide the chest wound. It had been easy to remove his old clothes (a knife came in handy) but they couldn't get him into any others. Everything was too small for him, and besides they could barely lift him; he was as heavy as rock. So they just squeezed him into a pair of trousers with the fly gaping open – the zip didn't work – and left him like that. Perhaps that was why he'd apparently never worn them, for they seemed brand new. 'If they want him in the next world, they won't mind about an open fly,' Gocheto noted.

True, the other world wouldn't mind about an open fly; they wouldn't care about the lack of a shirt.

Indeed they wouldn't be so finicky as to cavil over the want of a soul. They would have him anyway. His soul had gone down where the others were, seeking the friends and relatives it had never met in this world. Even now it was exploring every dark corner, hoping to find them! But if it didn't, would it come back? It would not. Once you fall into the black hole, there you stay. Once you were something, now you are no more, whoever you might have been. In the kingdom of the dead you can roam as you please; no one can see you. (Not that anyone was very interested to see you while you were alive, come to that.) Yes, being alive was very fine, but being dead was twice as noble. What a sad thing that Sava had become so noble. For nothing, and in the blink of an eye. How could a man like that die so easily? Before he could turn round, he'd had it: a knife in the back. And who had stabbed him? One of them, a friend. And the killer did it so easily, more like a machine than a man, one unthinking stretch of an arm. But he could just as easily not have.

As he gazed at the corpse below he suddenly felt again the chilly slime on his body, and shivers up his spine. If the dragon had not discarded him in preference for another life, it would be he lying there instead... He was sick and tired, he had to get away while there was still time. While he was still alive. It was time he stopped choking on his fear and merely watching. After all, he was a man, wasn't he? Of course, the boy came first. So let him first save the boy and then himself. The child should keep his eyes wide open instead of turning a… blind eye to life like his father, preoccupied with everyday nothings. Life passed by and that was it. You've seen what you've seen, and no more, and that's it. But there was more, if you wanted there to be. You could close your eyes and make a wish, like a child when he sees a shooting star in the night sky. He closed his eyes and waited. And as he waited, he felt it: the wish was welling up in his breast and he felt a surge of strength and he opened his eyes – Sava's dead face. The living close the eyes of the dead; the dead open the eyes of the living. That's how it was. This was the truth, horrifying as it might be. Where did all these dead men come from? There were so many accidents: a man stabbed in the back, drunks frozen to death in the snow, others butchered, shot, strangled or beaten to death, as well as suicides, missing persons, and the stillborn…

Yes, they had to put the lid on now. Let him rest in peace. The boys had shaved him and combed his hair and trimmed his moustache, so he should be happy with that, even if his shoulders and arms remained bare. Big, white arms with bulging stiff muscles, outlined against the black blanket. The elbows touched the sides as if straining for space, because the allotted space was the same for all sizes of corpse: lead coffins come in one size only. Sava seemed resistant to going in more than partway. Yet the entire body had to be manoeuvred inside somehow – it didn't matter which way, so long as the lid closed. It was a strenuous business, but gradually more and more of him was squeezed in, until only his feet jutted out.

'Can't go in,' said Hesho, who had been trying to push the feet inside. He was wearing a clean white shirt, which made him look unusually smart and formal, despite the chain tattooed round his neck and the grubby knitted cap striped in red and green pulled over his head. He looked regretfully at the body and repeated, 'Just can't!'

'Move out the way,' Gocheto broke in, shoving Hesho aside.

He should have been in bed, resting. When the doctor examined him, he said the feet were cut to the bone, cleaned the wounds up and bandaged them. Then he left him in bed and told him to stay there. But the moment his back was turned, Gocheto got up, removed the dressings, poured a bottle of brandy over the soles of his feet and then re-bandaged them in his own favoured manky foot-wrappings. He pulled on a pair of gumboots and rose to his feet with a particularly foul and loud oath.

'Hold the coffin!' Gocheto commanded, and pushed Sava's bare feet in their big heavy boots with all his might. They bent slightly, but not enough to squeeze inside. Gocheto let go, took a deep breath and tried again. The bony, stone-hard legs seemed to retreat a little, then gathered force and kicked him back.

'Damn!'

A rat scurried under the tables in the morgue, stopped in the corner and turned round, looking directly at Vasil. He started, trying to remember where he had encountered those bulging eyes before. He was sure they were familiar – but after all, this was only a poor startled rat, and probably a hungry one too. It must have been looking for something to eat in the morgue. Rats follow people and feed on their leftovers, but when there aren't any leftovers they eat the people themselves. There was the well-known case of the baby left home all alone by its mother, and when the mother returned, the baby was gone; only rats remained, and they were freshly gorged ones... He had thought this was nonsense, a nasty myth, but looking at that rat in the corner now, with its wary predatory eyes flashing in the semi-darkness, he began to think it less fanciful. Here they had ready access to people – albeit dead people – that conveniently lay on the tables. When left alone, the rats would begin to crawl over them, perhaps nibble a forehead first, then munch an ear or two, and snouts would become progressively bloodied. He felt sick and unsteady, with an odd discomfort in his neck. He felt sure he was going to fall over and very likely wet himself. Then the rat turned back and scrambled through a gap in the wall. He took a deep breath and, though the air he inhaled was stale and scented by corpses, he felt better. He was perfectly steady on his legs now, but the desire to relieve himself remained. In fact, he realized, he hadn't relieved himself for two whole days! As he thought of this wonder, the pressure in his swollen bladder became worse. He'd have to have a piss, and pretty quick.

'We'll have to cut him,' Meto barked abruptly, startling Vasil back to reality. As he spun round he saw how brick-red Meto's scorched cheek was. When they'd cut his bonds before the police came, Meto hadn't said a word. He'd acted perfectly naturally and calmly, as if nothing had happened, gone straight to his room and hugged his beloved dog. Later, when the police captain asked him what had happened, he said sorry, he couldn't remember anything at all.

'With a saw, otherwise he won't go in. And they don't take them without a lid,' he explained, his voice echoing in the empty morgue.

'What d'you mean, with a saw?' Gocheto broke in.

'Just that – cut him with a saw. It's not as if he's got any blood left in him anyway.'

'He's a human being!'

'So what, he's dead, he's not going to feel anything. If *we* don't cut him *they* will, and God knows what sort of mess they'll make.' There was a pause while the possibilities were considered.

'Just how should we do it?' someone asked without enthusiasm.

'Dunno, but everything should be inside. Stuffed in and then closed.'

'The head,' Hesho declared, looking at the others with a satisfied expression. 'The head is easy to cut and it's just one thing. We'll stuff it between his feet.'

'Have it your way, do what you like – but don't cut the head off. You need your head in the next world just like you do in this one,' Gocheto said firmly.

'Maybe... but how do you know? Anyway, he's not going to the next world, he's going to Bulgaria.'

'Better to cut the feet. Better to have no feet than no head. We might be sending him to Bulgaria, but that's just the same as the next world, really,' Meto said sagely, wrinkling the scorched half of his face like an old turkey.

'Balls.'

They were all standing round the body staring at it. Vasil tried to imagine Sava with his head between his feet. It really did seem to belong on his shoulders, and death had fixed it there more firmly than ever. The bare throat with its bulging Adam's apple issued a sort of challenge, a mysterious self-confidence moulded by stiff masculinity. He noticed the small spots of shingles that dotted the neck. Sensing death beneath them, they were struggling to hang on to their own form of life. They were still purple, though now desperately swollen and parched on the white skin; but death was slowly coming to them too, as the once warm body they populated turned to ice. He felt an immoderate wish to dig them out. They were an ugly sight on the dead man, they slurred death, upset the integrity of its beauty. But though they might be removed, not so the head. He imagined it landing with a thump on the guardian angel, which had been placed beneath. Then tête and tapestry would be stuffed in together.

He couldn't take his eyes off the dead man, though painfully aware of his own bladder. There he laid, in the coffin, arched and bent, legs jutting out. The white ankles, too thin and delicate for his height, were visible in the gap between the black homespun trousers and the tops of the boots. They were expecting to be sawed off, one after the other, like branches trimmed off logs. Trees were easy to cut, but what about human beings? The people who inhabited Bulgaria in ancient times had done it. They cut the feet off their dead and buried them by their side so they wouldn't wander back to haunt their relatives of a night time. A primitive custom that had apparently died out many centuries ago, but shortly to be revived in this very morgue, it would seem. But as Sava didn't have any relatives, the logic rather fell away. It couldn't be proper to cut bits off someone just because he didn't fit into his coffin. It wasn't as if they'd asked him first. No, a man wasn't a tree.

'I'll get the chain-saw,' he heard Hesho say.

'Hold on!' he shouted. His voice startled him – surely it wasn't his? – But Hesho whirled round and was staring at him anyway.

'What's the matter?' he demanded to know. 'I'll cut him. I know how. I've castrated donkeys so I know about these things.'

'No, not like that. If we just heat him, he'll soften up,' he said as calmly as possible. 'That'll be better.'

He was hoping they'd get the idea right away, because he didn't have the strength to explain it to them. (There was also the urgent matter of his bladder.) But they simply couldn't hack him up, even if no one was ever going to open the coffin. After all, he was a worker like them, wasn't he? Yesterday they had been side by side, they had relied on him, splendid fellow that he was.

How could you cut his feet off the next day? You couldn't. At least, you shouldn't.

He felt he was about to piss himself; he could only just control his bladder and hold it all back. The cold was trying to squeeze it out, any minute now it was going to pour down and flood the floor of the morgue! He couldn't hold it back any longer – perhaps another second, just a split second! – And he turned round and rushed to the toilet.

He kicked the door open. A Russian in brown trousers, red plastic mac and a light blue patent leather cap occupied it. He was squatting bare-arsed, perilously perched over the hole. He looked drunk, but somehow kept his balance. Raising his head, he looked at his unexpected visitor with colourless eyes.

'Any paper?' he asked in Russian.

'Fraid not.'

'Arsehole,' the Russian said, then dipped between his buttocks, produced a hand with shitty fingers and wiped them on the wall.

Vasil stepped back and went into another cubicle, principally because he couldn't hold it back any longer, he had to relieve himself regardless, there and then. He couldn't see anything. He frantically unbuttoned his fly and immediately a torrent streamed out. Hot clouds of steam rose. The smell of bleaching powder and urine made his eyes smart and they filled with tears. He luxuriated in the emptying of his bladder, and almost felt born again. It was the most prodigious ejaculation ever, that stream he was shooting out. He suddenly wanted to be with his wife, the mother of his child. He was overwhelmed by real desire, wanted to have her body and gaze into her eyes, wide open and unfathomable, wanted to chew her nipples and bite her lips. Yes, if he could get to her he was going to violate her, brutally, again and again, making her pregnant each time, fathering innumerable children... they'd spread all over the world, and make it a better place. And she'd feel it all right, and she'd enjoy it too – lucky her, he'd make her happy, very happy, the happiest woman of all, the happiest mother of all! Ah, yes... Not right now, no. But there was still time and the right time for everything, no one could stop you. (Except death of course, waiting patiently back in the morgue.) There he stood, a real man – legs apart, fly open, poised over the deep toilet hole, splashed in piss and curiously horny, all alone in that toilet cubicle. Then he buttoned himself up, fastened his belt tight and banged the door shut behind him with his elbow.

'Arsehole!' came a voice from the adjacent cubicle.

He walked back into the morgue and caught a whiff of almonds. It seemed to come from the corpse, but it had been there long before, lingering low under the bare tables. He could smell it deep in his nostrils.

The others had dragged in an iron stove with a pipe that had been pushed through the open window, and they were standing around it in a circle. Stuffed with logs, the stove crackled and smoked, and resinous wafts repeatedly ignored the ventilation provided and rose toward the ceiling.

'Give us a hand, will you? Let's put him on the stove.'

They gripped the coffin on all sides. The metal edges cut into his fingers, but he tried to ignore the pain, he couldn't let go even though he wanted to. The stove was close, just a few steps away, they just had to turn and – there it was. The coffin was heavy, but so surely was Sava, as if he was made of lead too.

'Damn him, he's heavy!'

'That'll be because his soul's gone.'

'Ah, that must be it.'

They had placed it on the small round plate of the stove. Though it looked kind of wobbly, actually nothing was going to make it fall off. It was now just a matter of time before it heated up sufficiently. So they gathered round the stove, waiting and warming themselves.

'Wonder if he will soften up,' Gocheto said, reclining on one of the morgue tables.

'Takes a while,' Meto replied.

'Hope it's not too long, or his beard will grow. Men grow beards even when they're dead.'

'They do, but what difference does it make?'

Hesho fumbled under his shirt, produced a candle and lit it with a match. He pushed the candle between the fingers of the dead man, so it would burn by the open window.

Suddenly Vasil saw her again, Yaskata's wife, in the flame of the candle over the dead man. She was kneeling toward the window with her back to him; her hair combed back, her dress skin-tight as before. He didn't know if she was weeping or smiling, but it was impossible not to keep looking at her. By degrees she turned till her profile was disclosed, and he saw that familiar face – not Yaskata's wife, but his own wife. He closed his eyes.

When he opened them again she had gone, and the naked flame illuminated only the locked hands of the dead man. There was nothing else to be seen.

In a corner at the other end of the room, a shadow moved. He waited breathlessly for something like a dragon to reappear, but what he recognized were the flashing eyes of the rat. It scrambled around the oven, vanished behind the coffin for an instant, and then popped out on the other side, near the dead man's head. It stopped under the table Gocheto was lying on and bared its sharp, long fangs. When it gave a squeak, even though it was so slight a noise you could hardly hear it, the sound shot through Vasil's body like electricity, jolting him.

'Get out of here!' Hesho shouted, and stamped his foot. The rat jumped, scurried under more tables and slipped out under the door. 'I'll kill you!' he threatened. 'Damned vermin! Too many of them. They should all be killed or castrated. It'd clean the Earth up a bit.'

'There are certainly lots of them,' Gocheto confirmed, staring up at the ceiling.

'There always will be. We castrate donkeys, we should castrate other things too.'

'We don't castrate donkeys in our village. We only have male ones, too.'

'I'm sure your women must enjoy themselves,' Hesho leered, as he scratched a boil on his back.

'Our women have their men at home,' said Gocheto, with some dignity.

'Not the one I'm talking to, though.'

A sudden gust of wind blew in through the open window and extinguished the candle.

'Shit, it's dark!'

Night had long since fallen. They stood quietly in the semidarkness of the morgue, waiting for the fire to heat the corpse and soften up the flesh so it could be squeezed into the coffin. The fire in the oven burnt brightly, lighting up the room in scarlet, and they could all feel the heat. The first stars peeped curiously through the open window, but they were too far away to do anything useful.

Sava lay peacefully, patiently enduring the heat under him. Any moment, you thought, he'd sit up, face them and complain, 'Come on, stop playing silly games, it's fucking hot in here!' But no, he remained as he was, motionless, although it was indeed extremely hot. He pictured himself lying there instead of Sava, under the black blanket, arms folded. It was easy to imagine the heat doing more than softening the body, rather scorching it, the terribly hot metal cauterising flesh, the air filling with the stench of burnt human meat...

He took a deep breath and smelt it as he had imagined it.

'He's burning!' Hesho cried out, plunged forward and gripped the coffin. But he immediately let it go again.

'It's fucking hot!' he screamed and spat on his palms. He removed his white shirt and the voluptuous mermaid tattooed on his shoulder reappeared. He tucked the bundled shirt under the coffin and glared at the others.

'Come on,' he urged. 'Lift him! Not with bare hands, though.'

Gocheto took a suitable log from those awaiting the fire, shoved it under the coffin and, holding the other end, gave the word.

'Now!'

Between the four of them, they lifted the coffin and replaced it on the table. It had caved in slightly in the middle, and there was a hole.

'It's bent!'

'Will the lid still fit?'

'Yes, it's only a bit bent.'

They relit the candle and fixed it on the edge of the table, then turned Sava onto his front, still in the coffin. His back was not badly burnt – there were charred holes in the blanket, especially around the buttocks, and in the trousers, but the skin was almost intact. They left him like that for a while, so he'd heat up from both sides. Then they rolled him back.

Gocheto gripped the head and neck. Hesho grasped the feet, made little progress, then tried standing on tiptoe to increase the leverage, but achieved no more success and gave up.

'We'll get him in,' he declared. 'Hang on a minute, though.' He stepped forward, clasped the corpse under the armpits and pulled it up as far as he could.

'Can you hold him for a bit?' he asked Gocheto, then pulled the white shirt from under the coffin and slipped it over the dead man. 'He won't be properly dressed, but he can have something anyway. Later on he'll be able to put it on himself. Could be a bit small for him... but at least it's clean, even if it's not ironed. I've hardly worn it since I washed it.' Then he turned to address the shirt's new owner.

'Put it on if you want to,' he said matily, and slapped Sava on the chest, quite hard.

Vasil thought Hesho might well be crying, but he couldn't see very well, since Hesho quickly drew back, lowered his head, grabbed the feet, and (with some extra reserve of strength he appeared to have tapped) this time strained and squeezed them into the coffin.

Sava lay much as he had before, but with his knees bent slightly. He looked like a young child, cold and huddling under the blanket, lulled to sleep by the bedtime story of a mother who had lovingly tucked him in before leaving the room, and would wait for him to wake up so she could again take him in her arms. But his mother wasn't there, indeed no one had even heard of her.

It was they who were there, just a few people randomly raked in from the rest, with a doubtful past and more doubtful future, as close together as mice who had all been caught in the same trap.

'Let's close him. It's late,' Meto said in a flat voice.

'Just a sec,' Gocheto said, and limped out of the morgue.

Meto turned round, and the candle lit up his burnt side. He was crying soundlessly.

There was Mario in the candlelight, running through a field dotted with red poppies, gazing up at the sun with his arms flung out. He had to save him before another coffin lid would be closed.

Gocheto came back. He had quickly gathered some alder twigs, some of which he laid by Sava's head; others were strewn over the body.

'No flowers,' he muttered in explanation.

Vasil was uncomfortably aware that he also should have given Sava something or else told him something, perhaps words of consolation, or inspiration. Something useful. There was, of course, the question of deciding which audience you were speaking to. If all else failed, one could simply say 'Farewell!' He had just decided he was going to say that, when someone else said:

'Now!'

And the lid closed shut. All that lingered on was a stillborn *farewell* on the tip of the tongue. Death departed, and life remained. Cruel old Charon was already leading the dead man's soul far down below, along the troubled waters of Acheron, towards the kingdom of the dead, while in the living world above, a final requiescat:

'Aw, fuck it.'

The candle was blown out.

He was just lying there in the dark, too tired to do anything. As soon as he'd got back to his hut he'd fallen onto the bed, without bothering to take any clothes off. He'd imagined he would drop off to sleep within seconds. But no, he remained wide-awake, staring into the darkness. He'd spent other nights alone, but he had never before felt loneliness as something so hellishly dense and saturated. When Yaskata had slept across the room the loneliness had been mitigated by the presence of another living person. Now there was no one there – only the bare bed of a murderer, one of many murderers. He'd deliberately left the lamp unlit, not feeling up to confronting the scene in all its vivid horribleness. He knew everything would be just as they'd left it, with all the mess and splinters, blood-spattered and brandy-soaked.

Had Lida stayed she might have tidied up, but she'd quickly got dressed and scarpered with the child before the police came. She was already in enough trouble with the law as it was, so no one thought of stopping her or asking her where she was going. The men, and he with them, had pretended to be so preoccupied with the dead man that they didn't see them leave the room. Fear, which ought to have been shared equally between all of them, was absorbed by the woman and the child alone, and when they left, it went with them. Then they were forgotten.

Quite where she could have gone with so young a child in such a night, after everything that had happened, God alone knew, and He was unlikely to provide an answer. But they would have found some place or other, a temporary haven where they might shelter from pursuit. Wouldn't they?

The little girl was at the centre of his troubled thoughts, even if she seemed strangely un-fragile and even if the dreams she dreamt awakened death – or perhaps because of that. It was obvious that he shouldn't have let them go like that, like ghosts. For a while his feelings had been dulled, but now he felt his guilt painfully: he had done nothing about the little girl and her mother. He had done nothing to help the little girl. On his sleepless bed, he kept thinking this.

He must do something for the girl and for his son and for everybody, he vowed feverishly. Instead of remaining uselessly guilt-ridden, good only for watching and listening as everything happened. Just as his son would go blind, the girl would become a whore like her mother. Before long, some drunk with too many hormones would be ripping through the outward innocence she still possessed. She must have lost the inward sort soon after she was born. And this would be the beginning of it: pain would turn to pleasure, pleasure to lust, lust to routine, routine to death.

Even if no one had bothered before, he wasn't prepared to let it happen. He would block its way, or at least try his damnedest, and not sit back full of noble compassion but as useful as frozen slush. He had come to love this child, as a father would. And if he was not her father, now, what man was? Someone had to hold out a guiding hand and lead her along the narrow path of life to some better place than this, somewhere to the south – God alone knew where, but it could hardly be worse. Someone like himself.

He had always agreed that he wanted a son. And when Mario was born, he told his wife and everyone else how happy he was that his wish had been granted. But it wasn't so. If he had been unsure before his son was born, he was sure afterwards that what he really wanted was a daughter. (In fact he would rather Mario had been a girl, but never said that to his wife, and rarely said it to himself.) Sometimes at night he would see if he could persuade his wife to try again. He had some thought that a second child might save their marriage and inject some purpose into their sterile life together. But she always rejected the idea, saying that the experience with Mario had been enough for her. After Mario fell ill, the subject was never mentioned again. All they thought about was the one child they had, the fruit of a love grown cold. In his feeble eyes they saw their guilt, the guilt of dead love that paralysed their bodies, clouded their thoughts, and scratched their consciences.

This was the only nexus between their lonely destinies. At night, avoiding each other's faces, they would stare at their shadows, futilely trying to gain some idea of how it had all soured between them, and at just such times they would hear his sobs on the other side of the wall – easy enough to hear, but far from easy to understand. They wondered why he cried, why he woke up at night, why his eyes were failing; but they wondered in silence, terrified that if the answer were spoken their blame would be revealed and impossible to obscure ever again.

Well, the next time he wouldn't be asking questions or giving answers; not like that. He was going to march in and hurl the bed covers on the floor, rip all her clothes off, laying naked all her doubts and fears as he did her soft body, and then give it to her good and hard, until she screamed in agony, until he made her give him a daughter like herself. And who was to say that her private demons wouldn't be expelled at the same time? So let her scream and moan while he ploughed into her (as a husband was entitled to), it would be good for her, and later she'd realize it and be grateful, she'd stop sobbing and see sense. And later still she'd be suckling his little daughter with her thick, sweet, scented milk. And him too, there'd be plenty to spare. Her breasts were so big… and even more so after childbirth, when they were heavy and engorged with milk. After Mario she'd tried pumping it out to ease the pressure, but almost as soon as she had, it was flowing again, more and more of it, forming two wet circles on her bra. For months on end it continued flowing, seemingly enough to feed all the hungry babies in the world. There was nothing to be done but pour most of it down the sink. Yet this was all being produced for one very small baby that struggled to find the nipple and cried and grimaced in frustration when it failed to.

No, Mario couldn't get his bearings even then, but at the time they didn't understand why not, and they more or less laughed it off. The reason, they thought, was that his sight was just a little slow, and they helped it along by shaking a rattle over his head. Had they done something wrong? Or had someone given him the evil eye? No one could say. But years later, they were trying a surgeon instead of a rattle. The surgeon cost 5,000 roubles more than the rattle, but it wasn't at all certain that he'd be any more successful. It was the price of a grain of hope.

He would earn what was needed, but it was a race against time; the danger was that he would return with the money just too late, when it would be useless and no doctor could help. It was a rough, brutal path he was trying to run, often hard to follow; sometimes you might well doubt there was a path at all. Now and then you lost your way in the darkness and tottered on guided only by instinct, unable to see where your steps were falling; you might sense you were about to plunge into an abyss and, rightly or wrongly, strike out in another direction. But where this route would take you was impossible to know. You might be going round in circles, or backwards. He'd had this feeling even on the train, before he arrived. He thought he was going to be sick. He opened the window and the wind rushed in and curled up beside him. He looked out and saw the high floodlit wall of the prison running alongside the railway track. Something about the wind and the prison wall gave him a presentiment, and he shut the window. Then on the bus, he'd sat where he sat, and others sat where they sat. Some were chosen by death in the accident, while those like him who'd missed death journeyed on, but he never saw them again and before long he'd forgotten who they were. He soon forgot the dead, too (excepting himself). He carried on with his dead man's walk, which was bound to go nowhere and had brought him to this place of tired railway trains and rusting men.

Sava's corpse was pointing the way. Dead men's bodies, no longer needed by their previous owners, were often good guides. The main thing was to stay alive, for you couldn't do much otherwise. It was strange that men enjoyed killing each other as they did, when there was really no hurry. In time, Death would take care of everyone. But two men had enacted this foreshortening before his very eyes. And when one of them died, a third man ran away. A third man with a blind child. As soon as he'd come to his senses, he'd bolted from the scene, a frightened animal.

Now Sava's bed was empty but his coffin was full. They had only just closed it; they had barely managed to squeeze him into that too-small space. A coffin was supposed to be the right size for a man. That coffin had been intended not for Sava but for him. He would have fitted nicely inside: no question of sawing or heating or squeezing. For a second time Sava had displaced him, just as he had when the logs crashed down, only this time he hadn't managed to save himself.

Thank God his heart had kept going. If he'd snuffed it then, who would have taken care of his son? Not his wife, who could only wring her hands and weep – not that one could expect much more from a woman on her own, naturally. The child would be lost and would never be saved... So many times had these thoughts recurred that their passage was as sure as water through an old channel. Yet even these most familiar pains were now flooded by the headache that thumped in his temples, then spread into his spine and filled his whole body. It merged with the darkness and engulfed the room and squashed his loneliness into every corner of the hut, for the pain, while it was there, was yet more insistent.

Later, when his senses had cleared, he was sure he heard something ominous, something moving outside the hut. Possibly a dragon returning to claim a human soul it had narrowly missed before. He strained his ears in anticipation. All was silent again. It had not been a sound made by a dragon though, but by a human. A hurrying, scurrying sound, the sort made by someone up to no good. If it was the convicts, he was done for. They didn't think twice, they'd slit your throat as soon as look at you, like wild animals aware only of the need to survive. And his hut was closest to the forest, the first they'd see. But he wasn't Old Igor – he didn't have any vodka and he didn't have any money. So what could they expect to get? All he had was his life and that wasn't worth very much. Still, it was worth something to him.

He reached for the gun hidden with its ammunition under the mattress, pulled it out and pushed a cartridge into the breach. Then he sat up and leant against the wall, waiting. The door creaked open, but there was no one there. His finger remained half-pressed on the trigger.

'It's me.'

It was the voice of a friend. He lowered the gun and allowed himself to relax. Now he could make out the silhouette, and saw it creep in silently as a ghost, go to the bed and sit down on it. He himself was of a piece with the darkness, invisible but filling the room with the noise of his thumping heart, ripped out from its victim. Then even the raucous heart became subdued as he heard the voice ask:

'Shut the lid?'

'Yes', he replied softly. The silence was impregnated with grief and balefulness, and not lightly broken.

'We knew each other for ages,' Yaskata started to say. 'I went to prison just before he got out. He'd run over a two-month-old baby in a box on the road. Later the police found out the baby's parents had left it there just so that would happen. But he still had to pay for its life. That's why he came here. And so we happened to meet again and we sort of got used to each other.'

He stopped and all was quiet as before. Vasil didn't know what to say, so he laid the gun aside, got to his feet and struck a match to light the lamp.

'Don't, they'll see me!'

'No they won't,' he told him and lit the wick.

The light scattered and burnt the darkness to ashes, caked blood and splintered glass strewn on the floor. He fumbled in his pocket and retrieved the old snapshot he had kept after they found it in Sava's bag. He held it out to him in the light of the lamp. Yaskata took the photograph and stared at it in bewildered recognition. He remained like that, speechless and blank, in the light that fell across his face. His good eye twitched, contracted and dropped a hot, bitter tear, which rolled down and dried on his cheek.

'He could have told me. Why didn't he tell me?'

'I don't know,' he said dully, raised the shade of the lamp and snuffed the wick.

They lay in their beds without saying anything, and the darkness and the silence lay there with them, embracing and alluring as death. When his eyes had got used to the dark, he saw Yaskata get up, reach under his bed and pull out a package. He came over and sat beside Vasil, and put the package down.

'Money. Take it, it's eight thousand – not much, but better than nothing. I saved it for the kids. They're still young, but they'll grow up. When they have, find them for me and give it to them. If you gave it to them now, their mother would just take it and spend the lot.' He said all this quickly, without taking breath, as if the sooner he was done with it the better. Then he added more slowly: 'I won't ever see them again.'

The money lay there, and he only had to reach out and take it – all of it – and keep it. Of course it wasn't his money, it had been earned by the pain and sweat of another man. But he was going to use it regardless for his own son. It was an opportunity, whether granted by God or by the devil (as if it mattered), and he had to take it before it was too late. Once the boy had been cured, he'd replace the money so these other children could receive their intended last gift, a legacy from another good-for-nothing father who had lost his soul. He would find them, wherever they were, and let them know how it was. 'That's from your father. Don't blame him for anything, he never had a chance.'

'What about you?' he asked the shadow that sat there quietly so close to him, almost indiscernible from everything else engulfed in the darkness of the night.

'There's an old man who ran away from the war and hid in the forest, as far away from the world as he could.'

He remembered the old hunchback who had forgotten how to talk but had managed to scare him into turning back from death. Since then he knew the forest trails were only for animals, and a man who followed such a path would end up dead or an animal himself.

'I've met him,' he heard himself say.

'I'm running away from the war too. There's no point in it.'

He watched Yaskata rise to his feet, pick up the gun and an ammunition belt and move to the doorway, where he paused, turned and said something.

By the time Vasil realized it had been *farewell*, his friend had gone.

In the morning, he was woken from a deep sleep by voices outside. He got up, went to the door and opened it. The sunlight rushed in and dazzled him, but as his eyes adjusted he saw that everyone was up and ready for work, hanging about in groups and chatting to kill time. After holidays everything started later than usual, including the trucks that drove you to the site. Meanwhile the usual lot, or most of them, were crouching down and exchanging boasts in the lee of the hut.

'As soon as I get back I'm going to build a house, and it'll be the best house you ever saw,' Gocheto was telling the others. 'Once you've got a house like that, you don't need to sweet-talk a woman to come, she'll be keen enough, and once she's there, she's there to stay. A woman needs children and she needs a man to father them! That's what it comes down to. Otherwise, what's the point? The thing is, I love children and I reckon I can manage a few more yet. And if that camel comes along again, I'll tie him to a tree in the garden so the children can see what a hundred-year-old hare looks like and play with him.'

'As long as you're alive you make mistakes, you know,' Meto remarked after Gocheto had finished.

'As long as we're alive, we'll get by somehow, then we'll see,' Hesho said.

'Wasting our lives, we are.'

Gocheto rose and went for the mail. If there was any, it was always delivered early in the morning, before they went to work. All the men eagerly anticipated it, secretly hoping that this time someone would have written to them.

'Letter for you,' Gocheto said, handing Vasil an envelope.

He took it from him and swallowed hard. News at last, after ages without. He would have written to them soon anyway, to tell them everything was okay and the hard times would soon be behind them. There wasn't much else he could say. He wanted them to pack their things and come; he'd meet them and they'd find the doctor and then there'd be nothing more to worry about. Nothing but a bad memory they could safely look back on. Even that would be good; it would bind them all the more tightly together. He'd write to them straight away, or as soon as he'd read the letter. She hadn't written to him for so long, he'd probably have trouble reading her handwriting.

'The crows are now crowing, soon it will be snowing,' someone observed sagely.

'Fuck all in the mail, it'll probably hail,' suggested another.

But in truth the weather seemed set fair. The sun was due to rise shortly, although it didn't seem in any great hurry. Frost continued to bite and benumb the ground, but a thaw was expected unless the crows were to be believed. He tore open the envelope and took out the sheet of paper. Spread out, it retained the impression of a cross from its folding.

There was no salutation.

I don't know the best way to write this letter, so I'll be brief and hope you will understand. The way things are, the earlier you know the better it will be for everyone. I love you and I always have done. But I have decided to leave you and you must give me a divorce. While you were away, I met a Greek man who owns a hotel and a lot of shops. He asked me to marry him and promised to arrange for Mario to be treated in the best hospital in the West, and I accepted his offer. Any mother would do the same. I know that you have done your best, but it just isn't enough and the child will go blind unless something else is done. I would never forgive myself if that happened. I know you will blame me, but I am doing it for Mario's sake. Please try to understand and, if you can, forgive me. I am waiting for your consent and hope everything will be as painless as possible for both of us.

Elena

He felt terror, a primitive terror of death. Then nothing except the urge to die. And he stumbled away, across Scrap Town and into the forest. He walked and walked, blind and deaf and dumb. He walked for a long time, until he fell and sank onto the ground.

When he came to, there was no one else there. Only lingering images of the loving wife, the healing child, the blessed family – a lost hope, a dream that now could only come true for another man. He lay there alone, helpless, with sand coating his tongue and gritting between his teeth. All that he saw through his half-closed eyes was blurred and chimerical: trees that bent down to tear the earth with scrabbling claws, frantic for water; then shafts of sunlight which scurried over the moss and played with the branches, first teasing them maliciously, then relenting as they stayed and warmed. As lesser rays were guided onto his body he began to experience calmness, a sense of nature embracing and explaining and dissolving everything. He let go the sure thought that this was an illusion that would not last.

The earth beneath was in sympathy, absorbing his tiredness, the forest was still, and only the dull thumps of his heart echoed in his ears. Gradually he became aware of another rhythmic beat that came from outside him. Looking round, he saw a large animal a mere stone's throw away. His first, wild thought was: 'The Arcadian stag! But what is it doing here – especially as no-one's chasing it?' A moment later he saw it for what it was, a common elk, banging its big, thick horns against a tree to shed them. It kept twisting its head and struck hard and repeatedly until its burden was shed, and then vanished into the forest and he saw it no more.

He got to his feet and then followed the trail of the deer, on and on till it took him to the river. He stepped into it and immediately the icy coldness shot through him, paralysing him for a moment. The current streamed between his legs, surging toward the ocean but destined to freeze first. He waded out farther and followed his reflection, which was always lying on the surface of the water, just ahead. Eventually it became distorted, then disintegrated and vanished in the deep memory of the river. He turned round and wandered somewhere else, with no guide or purpose. He had decided that he was going to die, exhausted, sooner or later to be devoured by beasts, when he noticed that his body had instead decided to return to Scrap Town.

Now emptied of workers, the place seemed as derelict as the gnawed bones of a skeleton. He could see no one except for two human figures, sitting in silence on the logs in front of his hut. Mother and child huddled by a pile of ashes; all that remained of the fire had burned out long before. They looked as if no longer alive, flesh cold but souls still fettered, long inured to the death of their bodies. But when he approached, the smaller figure came to life, coming to meet him with hands outstretched. He looked into her eyes, and they were the same eyes the dream had escaped from, but now they were open and innocent as freshly gathered flowers. Before he could think what to say she had grasped his hand and was pulling him after her. Big snowflakes had begun falling, melting as soon as they touched the ground to leave no trace. But they were compelled to keep falling.

The mother had followed. She stopped them with a question, as she hunched over what little the crows had left of the dog.

'Who are you? – You that ain't never had me.'

'No-one.'

'Well you don't belong here anyway.'

'What about you – where do you belong?'

'I belong here all right. Where men are, where they die,' she said and their eyes met and he understood it was the simple truth.

'What about her?' he asked, and looked at the girl. She was still holding his hand, clinging on as if otherwise she would be lost.

'Her? You can have her.'

The little hand gripped him so tightly that it hurt and brought him back to life.

A jeep suddenly appeared on the muddy road, swung into the empty square and crunched to a halt. A lean figure in a black jacket and leather boots got out and walked confidently toward the little group.

'So we're going to play daddy, are we?' the foreman mocked, in his half-spitting way. 'And who's gonna do the work in your place? One died, another pissed off, and now you're gonna stick it in sweetie here. You're so keen to be the first; you want to make it good and early? Too bad. You go and work like you're paid too. I might just take care of this so-pretty little girl myself, and do it properly.' He treated the girl to an evil smile. She cowered behind Vasil's back, always keeping tight hold of his hand. It felt as if she was squeezing him with strength supernatural for one so slight.

He was overwhelmed by fear, the familiar fear that all his life had pushed him back and stolen his strength as in dreams. The fear of a beaten dog, bleeding and wounded, tongue lolling out, and death very close. He felt her hand in his, a warm little hand, imploring his protection and gripping so tight that it hurt. Her warmth and her strength passed into him; the anger from her poured through his veins and ignited the heart that had grown cold and numb. Alchemy changed his fear into fury, and the hatred that was burning in his soul blocked out everything else.

He let go her hand. He let go his conscience. He had nothing to be troubled by, least of all his life, absurd as it was. Death entered his chest, and his shoulder, and his arm, and his fist. With a force that was not human, a force created by vengeance and despair, his hand lifted, swung back, amassed a weight of pain, and crashed it down on the man in front of him. The wretched foreman was driven into the ground as if he had fallen from a height, and whatever soul he might have possessed fled his body. Splayed on his back, he gazed up with mousy eyes that were already losing their brightness.

A crow that had eaten dog too long ago perched on the jeep, and then another.

'They're good boots,' the woman said thoughtfully.

Vasil lifted the child into his arms and carried her with his borrowed strength to where the train stood, already snorting steam and gearing up to be gone. The heavy shafts hissed into life, at first jerkily and then with confidence, compelling the massive rusty wheels to turn. Slowly but unstoppably the train moved forward, gathering momentum all the time.

He had to run, and as he did the wind blew the child's hair against his cheeks. When he caught up with the train it was moving as fast as he could run, and it was all he could do to put the girl on the very last step. He saw her stretch out her hand to him, and then he collapsed onto the cold, hard ground.

It was an old train and knew the way well enough. It snaked along its own trail, obscured by the taiga, the swamps and the white night, but betrayed by the sound of its heavy wheels.